A Simple Change

Amish Wedding Season Book 5

Samantha Price

Second Edition 2015

ISBN 978-1500119539

License Notes

Table of Contents

Chapter 1

And if a house be divided amongst itself,

that house can not stand.

Mark 3:25

It seemed like a good idea to him at the time of purchasing, but now Richard Black had taken possession of his old Amish family home, he realized that he had bitten off more than he could chew. He knew nothing of renovating houses and prior to joining the community, he had lived in either apartments or houses that were modern and fitted with the latest technology. It was purely a sentimental whim that led him to purchase the old *familye haus*. After he had a closer look at the home, Richard was certain that this sentimental whim was going to end up to be nothing but a huge money pit.

As he stomped his way through the house, he was daunted by the amount of work that needed to be done. His only knowledge of house renovation came from watching late night house flipping shows on television when he couldn't sleep. It certainly looked easy on the shows, but now that he was surrounded by crumbling plaster, damp spots, and rotting floorboards, he was not so sure that renovated would be as easy as it looked.

His mind jolted to his own family and the fact that he was the sole remaining Black of his lineage. He had a brother, but his brother had changed his last name giving the explanation that Black was a negative name. He wondered if he would die without children to carry the Black name. At least he had made a step toward preserving something of his heritage, by purchasing the old house.

I've been so caught up with making money and being successful that I've forgotten what's really important. He wondered what drove his grandmother to leave the community when she was sixteen since she would have had a loving family and was part of a close-knit community.

Was any man worth leaving all that for? He wondered if she ever regretted her decision. That was something he would never know. All he knew was that she told him a little of the Amish and how they lived. She told him stories of a barn raising and told him stories of the Amish weddings. *She did say that her wedding was just herself and grandpa, no guests and no one they knew.*

Musty air filled Richard's nostrils as he walked slowly through the empty rooms. The stale air, and the fact that everything was covered in dust, told him that the house had been uninhabited for some time.

Well, I wanted a new life and here I am, slap bang in the middle of it. He banged a hand on the wall and as he did plaster dust fell all over him. He jumped back, dusted himself off and sneezed. After he sneezed a couple times he noticed that white dust was falling out of his hair.

Putting new surfaces on the walls would be another thing on the ever growing list of things to do. If it hadn't been an old family home, it would be much more economical to pull it down and start afresh. He wouldn't do it though, not to an important historical building, such as this.

He leaned against the posts of the front door, and looked across his land. He had no idea what to do with all of it. He was no farmer, that was for sure and nor did he desire to be one. *I'll most likely have to lease it to someone,* he thought. *I'll have to have a look at that cottage too and see what I can do with it. Maybe I can lease that out as well.*

His gaze traced the landscape, following the gentle undulations and small clusters of trees scattered here and there.

There was an abundance of birds that had not stopped tweeting since sun up. They sang songs as they flittered about the overgrown garden, which surrounded the *haus*. Richard ventured out into the garden and picked up a blade of grass popping the end into his mouth; he turned his face up to the sun.

A sense of belonging overwhelmed Richard as he stood looking over the land that belonged to his family.

According to the Amish genealogist the Bloughs built the house over two hundred years ago. The last Blough to live in the *haus* was Enid Blough. Richard assumed that Enid must have been his maiden great aunt.

He turned his back to the land and looked up at the grand house and wondered what his grandmother's life was like growing up in this house. She ran away at sixteen to marry his grandfather but that did not mean that she was not happy; she ran away for love, to be with an *Englischer.*

A smile played upon Richard's lips as he admired his grandmother's sense of will and determination; it reminded him a little of his own drive.

It must have been a big decision at sixteen to leave the closeted life she knew to enter a life she knew nothing of, he thought.

A movement in the distance caught Richard's attention. A tiny figure appeared to be moving very quickly towards his house. He was sure it was a woman – yes, an Amish woman.

As she got closer, he saw that her dress was dark purple and she donned a prayer *kapp* and white apron. This was a woman that he did not recognize as being a part of the community. In fact, he was sure that he had never met this woman before. As she drew nearer, he could not take his eyes from her. She was proud - he could tell by the way she strode with purpose toward the house.

Richard knew he could read people well, something that came with being a money lender for many years and dealing with all kinds of people.

When Richard could see her face more clearly, he noted that if it were not for the sour expression on this woman's face, she might be an attractive woman indeed.

She stopped a few feet away from him. “You, Richard Black?” Her tone was fierce, and her stare blank.

Richard raised his eyebrows as his eyes swept over her slowly before he chose to speak. The messy hair poking out from her prayer *kapp* was light brown with streaks of gold. Her eyes were piercing blue; her skin was pale, and light freckles dotted her slightly upturned nose. Unsightly creases between her brows gave Richard the unmistakable information that this woman was mighty cross.

“Pleased to meet you, and you are?”

She cut across his words. “What do you mean by stealing my house?” She placed her hands on her hips.

Richard took a step closer to the woman.

“I have the deed to this house. I bought it fair and square at auction.” He narrowed his eyes concerned that there might have been some real estate funny business that would see him losing his house. *Maybe she has some kind of legal claim to this house that I don't know about,* he thought. The last thing he wanted was a legal battle. "Why is it that you say it's yours; and who the devil are you?"

The strange woman flung her arm in the air, toward the *haus*. "This home was my *mudder's* before she left it to me in her will."

"So, it was you they foreclosed on?"

Her dark blue eyes flashed with rage, as she said, "You stole it from me."

Richard had never faced an angry woman like this before – angry men yes, but never an angry woman. He wasn't sure what he should do. "Would you like to come inside and discuss it?" *Surely that would be the Amish way to solve a dispute,* he reasoned.

"It's my *haus*, how dare you invite me into my own home. You charlatan. You're in this with them aren't you?"

"Who? No, I'm not in anything with anyone. I bought this fair and square – as I said already." Richard wondered if this woman could possibly be a relative? There did not appear to be a family resemblance. "What did you say your name was?"

The woman almost growled with rage and yelled, "Because of you I'm living in a borrowed caravan on borrowed land. I have no home now because of you." She kicked dirt at him with her lace-up black boots. She glared at him for a moment before she marched back in the direction from which she'd come.

He noticed her hands were curled into fists.

Richard took a few steps back and watched walk away, just as he had watched her approach. "That's the most obstinate, unpleasant woman I've ever come across in my entire life," he murmured to himself. "Yet, I find her oddly appealing."

Chapter 2

I beseech you therefore, brethren, by the mercies of God, that ye present your bodies a living sacrifice, holy, acceptable unto God, which is your reasonable service. And be not conformed to this world: but be ye transformed by the renewing of your mind, that ye may prove what is that good, and acceptable, and perfect, will of God.

Romans 12: 1-2

"How dare he ask me into my own home. My home, not his."

"Betsy, calm down. Maybe he can't help it. He probably just bought it at the auction, not knowing what was going on."

Betsy forced a smile and nodded to her *schweschder,* Grace. "You always think the best of people, don't you."

"*Jah*, I think that's the best way. People are *gut* mostly. You seem to think everyone is bad, but they aren't."

Betsy nodded but only to appease Grace not because she agreed with her. She hoped that Grace would never have to find out just how awful some people could be, as she had. Betsy was the oldest of eight children and Grace was the youngest. There were ten years between Betsy and Grace, and even though Betsy was the eldest, she was the only sibling that had never married.

Betsy looked around her small caravan. She knew that she was supposed to be grateful for what she had, but how could she be grateful for this little caravan when she once owned and lived in a large home? Still, it was good of Grace's husband to allow her to have use of the caravan when she had lost her house. At least she could be close to Grace, and close to what was once her own home, which was on the parcel of land on the nextdoor property.

"I best be going, Betsy. Do you want to have dinner with us?"

"*Nee, denke*. I'll have dinner here." Betsy smiled on the outside, but on the inside she was fuming. Grace asked her to have dinner with her and her husband almost every day, and almost every day Betsy refused her kind offer. A tiny gas stove was all she had to cook on when once she had a large kitchen, and a beautiful blue-stone fireplace, larger than most every home in the County.

Through the small window of the caravan, she watched Grace walk the small distance, back to her *haus*. Grace and her husband shared the small home which once belonged to Betsy's *mamm* before she inherited the Blough *haus* from old Enid Blough.

Betsy often searched her mind for memories of the woman whose *haus* she used to call her own. She did remember that she used to go there when she was small, to play in the garden.

Enid Blough was a very kind lady and used to give her oranges to eat, and she was allowed to play with Enid's two small dogs. Once Betsy was old enough to go to school, she did not have much time to visit the old lady.

Then her memories jumped a few years to when Enid was old and feeble and Betsy's mother used to be gone often, looking after the old lady. As the eldest, Betsy would have to look after the children when her *mudder* was looking after Enid Blough. Sometimes when Enid was well enough, her *mamm* would send Betsy to visit Enid.

Betsy climbed up on the cramped single bed and looked up at the ceiling, which was very close. She was used to ten foot ceilings and this caravan roof was so low, that if she sat up in bed she would hit her head on the ceiling.

Her mind went to Richard Black and how he did not seem to care that he had stolen her house from underneath her. Now what was she to do? She would never be able to save enough money to buy another home. It seemed as if there was no point in going on with her life just to rot in this caravan.

Why continue with this life? I'm so old and I don't even have a home anymore. What is to become of me? Will I have to live in this van forever like some mad old woman? Maybe young children will spread rumors about me, that I'm a witch, she thought.

Betsy remembered the times she would walk to school past an old lady's house, she and her friend, Mary, would be scared of the old lady who lived by herself; they wondered if she might be an old witch. They used to walk very quickly past her place going and coming from school.

At least that old lady had a haus, not a caravan, she thought. *I will be the old witch that children are scared of who lives in a caravan.* At school Betsy had learned that gypsies live in caravans.

Children will say I'm an Amish gypsy witch and be fearful of me. If only the bank had stood by their promise when they said they would give me more time.

The bank called it a 'mistake' when she woke up to find a 'for sale' sign on her property, but that did not stop them from selling it out from underneath her.

It's people like that Richard Black who are ruining the world. They have plenty of money and they don't care who they tread on as long as they prosper. Well, two can play at that game, Mr. Black.

Betsy knew that she hadn't gotten married because she was too busy looking after her siblings to worry about her own happiness. It was only when her siblings began to get married, that Betsy considered that maybe she had been past over.

It wasn't that she was unattractive – she got compliments on her looks often so she knew that she was not awful to look at. She considered that the right *mann* had never shown up. No one had ever come calling and she had never been attracted to a man enough to consider dating or courting.

There had never been any man for Betsy to say ‘no’ to. After a while, she came to realize that marriage was not her lot in life. If it were then surely *Gott* would have provided the perfect man for her - is what she’d come to think.

Betsy had heard that the horrible, Richard Black, had recently been baptized into the Amish faith and was determined to leave his *Englisch* ways behind him.

Betsy knew she had a little money coming to her from the bank after the foreclosure sale, and maybe if she worked hard she could save enough to buy the house back, that is, if Mr. Black sold it cheap enough when he grew tired of living the Amish lifestyle.

And I can help him grow tired of being Amish, Betsy laughed and kicked up her heels in the air, careful not to touch the ceiling.

Chapter 3

Jesus saith unto him, I am the way,

the truth, and the life:

no man cometh unto the Father,

but by me.

John 14:6

Richard Black paused in the kitchen, and imagined how it would have been to live in the old house in years gone by, when it was filled with a family - the Blough family. He closed his eyes and put both hands against the kitchen sink.

He had learned that the kitchen was the hub of the activity in the Amish home, the place where the family would gather for their meals and chatter, exchanging details of their day.

Richard decided the best way to go about his renovation was to get opinions from experts; maybe call in an architect or two. He wanted to restore the old house to its original condition and do as much work on it himself as he possibly could.

Of course, he wouldn't be able to do any plumbing or electrical, but he was sure he could do any simple construction work. Construction work, he was sure, would be a welcome change from spending all day on his laptop or on his cell.

Richard, now in the living room, rubbed the stubble on his chin as he sat on an old wooden chair. The chair was the only furniture that had been left in the house. He surmised that since the house was sold at a foreclosure auction, it was clear that there was no value to the unusual looking chair or it would have been sold along with the other furniture.

"How could anyone have possibly lived here? It's a mess."

Richard bounded to his feet on hearing a voice at the door. It was Jakob Lapp.

"Jakob, come in," Richard said.

Jakob and Richard had once competed for Abigail Fisher who was now Jakob's wife. Since

Richard joined the community, Jakob had become a close friend.

"I asked a few people for you, apparently it wasn't always like this until recently. She was on her own and the repairs probably got the better of her." Jakob stood just inside the doorway and ran his eyes around the house.

Richard remembered the woman from the previous day who hadn't given him her name. It was not surprising to him that no one wanted to live with her and that she was on her own. "Do you know her name?"

"The woman who lived here?"

Richard nodded and leaned forward.

"Betsy Baywell." Jakob put his hand to his head. "She's an odd one."

Richard knew very well that she was an odd one, from first hand experience. He found it interesting that others thought so too. "What do you mean?"

"Oh nothing, pay me no mind. I spoke before I thought. I've been around you too long." Jakob laughed.

Richard pushed his jaw out and said, "You must tell me about Betsy. She came here accusing me of stealing her house."

A smile appeared on Jakob's face and he rubbed his *baard.* "I'll tell you what I've heard recently of the house. Old Enid Blough lived here; we know now that she was one of your relatives."

Richard nodded. "Yes that's right. Go on."

"She became sick, as often happens when people get older, and as she had no *familye*. Mrs. Baywell, from the next property, came and took care of her, cooked and cleaned for her, and did everything for her even though she had several *kinner* of her own to look after. When old Enid Blough died, she left the property to Mrs. Baywell who by that time was widowed."

"I see and Mrs. Baywell is Betsy's mother?"

"Was – Mrs. Baywell died some time ago. Betsy was the only *kinner* not married, so her *mudder* left the *haus* to Betsy."

"I see." Richard nodded slowly as he took it all in. "That still doesn't explain why the *haus* is in such bad repair. Wouldn't the community rally around and fix the place up for her – do a few repairs?"

Jakob shrugged his shoulders. "*Jah*, if the community knew about it they would've helped. I'd say no one knew the state of the place." Jakob tapped his boot against the rotting boards of the floor. "Betsy doesn't attend many meetings. She's quiet and keeps to herself."

"I guess that would explain the disrepair. What does she do to keep herself if she has no husband?" Richard knew that the Amish do not take welfare payments and without a husband she might have no way to support herself.

"I don't know. I haven't heard that she has a job or anything." Jakob adjusted his hat. "That's one question I can't answer."

"You didn't answer my original question, Jakob; which was, why do you say, or why do people say, that Betsy is a bit odd?"

"Nothing really, I guess. Just that she keeps to herself, like I said. No one seems to know too much about her. She comes to meetings about once every month, and hardly talks to people. When she does come, sometimes she doesn't even stay for the meal."

Richard slapped Jakob on the shoulder in a friendly manner. "I see. Thanks for telling me."

"I'm just glad we can be civil to each other now," Jakob said.

"Of course we can, you won Abigail fair and square. You were the one she wanted. I've no hard feelings whatsoever." It was a blow to Richard when Abigail told him that she was going to marry Jakob. He couldn't help but wonder if he'd joined the Amish earlier, maybe she would have chosen him instead of Jakob. Still, they had both become a support to him now that he was Amish.

"Have you decided what job you're going to tackle first?"

Richard looked about him with a downturned mouth. "At the moment, I'm just going to live in it for a while, as it is, until I can see what I want to do with it."

Jakob gave a chuckle.

"I know what you're thinking – everything needs doing, right?"

"Sorry, *jah*. It does look like everything needs fixing or replacing. Seems like it'll take a lot of time and money to bring it back to how it was."

Richard smiled. "Well, it'll be worth it. I hope."

"Abigail and I would like you to come to dinner tomorrow night."

"That would be nice. Tell Abigail I'll be there, *denke*." Since Richard had moved in, he found that the only thing in good repair was the gas stove. Cooking wasn't what he was best at.

He had eaten take-out nearly ever day since he had moved into the *haus.*

"What are you doing for transport?"

"I've been traveling by taxi since I sold the car." Richard did not like giving up the convenience of his car. He never thought he'd ever drive a horse and buggy, but now that he'd been without his own transport for some time he was looking forward to having his own horse and buggy. "Sorry, I can't ask you to sit down." Richard raised his hands in the air. "I don't have any furniture yet. One of could sit on the rocking chair."

Jakob laughed. "That's okay. Are you going to get a horse and buggy, eventually?"

Richard shook his head. "I'd like to, but I've never had much to do with horses except when I was staying with the Fishers."

"It's not hard. I could teach you if you'd like."

"When I was with the Fishers they showed me how to hitch a horse to the buggy and they taught me how to drive it. It's just the finer points of looking after a horse properly that I'd need to know."

"You can't use a taxi forever. There's not much to looking after a horse. When you're ready, I'll go with you to buy it, and the buggy too."

"You'd do that?"

"Of course I would."

"I'd appreciate that. I always wanted to have a horse – well that was when I was younger - when I was growing up."

After Jakob's visit was over, Richard watched his buggy disappear into the distance imagining what it would be like to have his own horse and buggy.

Suddenly, Richard felt alone. He had never given much thought about his childhood, but now it came flooding back to him. One emotion dominated his past, and that was loneliness. His parents were moderately wealthy and lived in a modest house. They did not like him to bring school friends back to the house so he had few friends while growing up.

As the sun shone on Richard's face, he wondered if his attraction to the Amish was their warm hospitality and friendliness. That was a thing that had been always sadly lacking in his life.

As he gazed across his land once more he noticed that his fences were all in good repair and certainly in much better repair than the house. The barn he had looked through earlier was in good repair. Richard wondered if he might be better off sleeping in the barn rather than the house.

Chapter 4

Have not I commanded thee? Be strong and of a good courage; be not afraid, neither be thou dismayed: for the Lord thy God is with thee whithersoever thou goest.

Joshua 1:9

The next night, Richard knocked on Abigail and Jakob's door. He was looking forward to a fine home cooked meal instead of another take-out.

"Richard, come in." Abigail met him at the door.

"*Denke*, for inviting me, Abigail."

Richard followed Abigail into the sitting room. Richard sank into the couch and looked forward to the time his house would be renovated so he could have a couch of his own to sink into. He would also be able to invite people to his *haus* for dinner as well. At the moment having people over for dinner seemed like a very long-range plan, given the current state of the house.

"Jakob says you're going to get a horse and buggy soon?"

Richard saw the twinkle of amusement in Abigail's eyes. "You're not mocking me Abigail, are you?"

"I'm sorry. I still can't believe you're Amish. The rich and successful Richard Black turns his back on the *Englisch* world to live a plain and simple life."

Richard laughed. "It might be plain, but not quite simple yet. I hope it'll be soon, when I get the *haus* fixed up."

"I must come around and see it. Jakob said it's very grand."

"Was once, I guess." Richard took the opportunity to get some history of the Blough residence. "Do you know or remember anything of the people who lived there?"

"Only what I've already told you. I remember an old lady living there on her own. Beyond that, I don't know anything."

"Do you know anything of Betsy Baywell?"

Abigail's lips twitched as she heard Betsy's name. "*Jah*, I know Betsy. She's a marvelous milliner."

"Milliner, hat maker? What sort of hats?" Richard tipped his head to the side, he'd never met a milliner before, and had never given much thought to the making of a hat.

"All sorts. She used to run Thomas' Hatmakers in town, before they closed down."

Richard brought his hand up to his chin. "When was that?"

"You mean, when did they close?"

Richard nodded.

"I think it was maybe about a year ago, why?"

"She used to live there in the house." Richard tapped his fingertips on his chin.

"Oh *jah*, Jakob told me. Did she accuse you of stealing it from her or something?" Abigail laughed.

Richard nodded again while thinking, *If Betsy lost her job that might explain why the bank had to take the haus, but surely that doesn't explain how the haus fell into such disrepair.*

At that moment, Tracy and Lizzy, Jakob's daughters from his first marriage, came into the room.

"Hello, Mr. Black." The two girls sat either side of him.

"Well, hello you two. How have you been?"

"Very well, *denke*," Lizzy said.

Tracy tapped him on the shoulder. "We're cooking the dinner for you tonight."

"*Denke*, that's *wunderbaar.* What are we having?"

The two girls looked at each other. "It's a secret," Tracy said, and then the two girls disappeared into the kitchen amidst a flurry of giggles.

"They certainly seem to be enjoying themselves."

"They have been a real delight to me. It's so lovely having young children around once more. I missed the laughter of children when mine grew up. Now I've got the *grosskinner*, but I don't get to see them everyday."

Richard wondered again if he would ever have children, if he'd ever know the joy of raising them.

"Would you like to have *kinner* some day, Richard?"

Richard threw back his head and laughed. "I must say I've never given it a lot of thought. I'd need a *fraa* first though, wouldn't I?" He did not want to share his longings with Abigail. There was no point in sharing his wishes with others.

Abigail nodded. "Are you looking for one? I could help you."

"You mean you could match-make for me, or something?" Richard leaned forward with his elbows on his knees and said in low voice, "You don't have anyone coming here to dinner tonight, do you?"

Abigail covered her mouth as she laughed. "I should have thought of that. *Nee*, I don't, but I could next time you come for dinner."

Richard hoped that Abigail would not ask him what type of woman he liked because he would have to say, a woman like her. Abigail had been his dream woman, attractive, intelligent and kind. Unfortunately, they weren't meant to be, at least that is obviously what Abigail thought when she chose to marry Jakob.

"So what about, Betsy?" Abigail leaned forward, her expression hopeful.

Richard leaned his back into the couch. "What about her?" He did not want to think about Betsy, let alone speak about her.

"She's a single woman, a little older than most of the single women in the community. She's attractive and smart too."

Richard slowly shook his head. "Just between you and me – I think she's the most objectionable woman that I've ever met in my entire life. She'd be the last woman I see myself with."

Abigail frowned. "*Nee*, I don't think she's like that. She was probably upset when you met her."

"How well do you know her?" Richard was sure he knew the answer. He was sure that no one in the community knew Betsy very well at all.

"I don't really know her. I've talked to her a few times at meetings and she seems nice."

Richard couldn't help but grunt. Nice was something that he knew Betsy Baywell was not.

Abigail straightened her back, tilted her head slightly, and said, "It can't be easy for her, to lose her *haus*. I don't know what I would've done if I'd lost my home and the two businesses. I was very nearly in her position not so long ago, remember?"

Richard nodded slowly as he recalled the recent problems that Abigail had faced.

"What I'm trying to say to you, Richard is, don't judge someone when you meet them for the first time. She's likely very stressed – she would feel as if she's lost everything. Very likely – she has."

Richard wondered whether what Abigail said was true. Maybe Betsy was only acting like a shrew because she lost her job then lost her house.. "I see what you're saying, Abigail. I think I've judged this woman harshly. Must be awful at her age to lose everything and have no husband, and no means of support."

Abigail straightened up and smiled. "*Jah.* Why don't you pay her a visit and sort out your differences?"

Before Richard could reply to Abigail, Jakob walked through the door. "Richard, you're here already. Come and see what I have in the barn."

Richard rose off the couch and followed Jakob into the barn, intrigued at what Jakob wanted to show him. He followed him right to the corner of the barn to a small fenced off enclosure.

"Want a puppy?" Jakob said.

Richard peered over the enclosure to see two puppies, playing with each other. When the puppies saw the two men they tried to jump out of the enclosure toward them.

Richard laughed at their clumsy antics. "They seem friendly enough."

"*Jah*, my dog had these two pups before we could get her spayed. The girls want to keep them both, but I said we could only keep one. We're going to keep that one, the female." Jakob pointed to the smaller of the two pups. "Abigail and I thought you might like to have the other pup for company."

Richard laughed. "Why would I want a pup?"

"You're all alone in that big *haus.* You need some company."

Richard studied the pups; it was obvious that they were not any particular breed. The mother was nowhere to be seen, but Richard recalled that she was a medium-sized dog. "How big will he grow?"

"Not too big, I'd guess." Jakob laughed a little. "I don't know who the father was, so it's just a guess."

Richard stepped into the enclosure and picked the male dog up. The puppy licked him all over his face while making running movements with his legs. "*Denke*, I think you might be right; a dog could be just what I need."

"Excellent." Jakob clapped his hands together. "He's ready to go tonight if you want, or you can come back in a day or two to get him."

"I think I'll take him home with me tonight, if that's all right."

Jakob smiled. "What will you call him?"

"Have you given him a name already?" Richard asked.

"The girls have been calling him Goldie, because of his color."

Richard wrinkled his nose. "I'll think about it, I don't know that I like the name Goldie."

"Well, best we get inside now. Dinner will be ready soon enough."

Richard put his dog down. "I'll call him, Max."

****

After dinner, Jakob drove Richard and his new puppy, Max, home. Richard made Max a bed out of blankets, next to his own. For the time being, Richard slept on a camping mattress in the largest bedroom. He still hadn't purchased any furniture, as he wanted to feel the mood of the house before he put money into the furniture.

To Richard's surprise, Max slept the whole night through, and as soon as Richard woke the next morning he took Max out on the grass. Max seemed to be house trained already, which Richard considered a bonus.

After a breakfast of scrambled egg made on the camping stove, Richard decided he'd pay Betsy a visit. Maybe he had misjudged her like

Abigail had said. They had definitely got off on the wrong foot and maybe he was partly to blame for that.

Either way Richard knew that he should not allow any root of bitterness into his heart. Bitterness is what he heard the bishop speaking about at the previous meeting the Sunday gone by. Richard was determined to follow all the ways of the Amish, which included living correctly according to *Gott.*

"Max, you're about to go on your first walk."

Max was chewing on a piece of wood that he brought in from the garden.

"And when we get this place fixed you won't be allowed to bring sticks in like that."

Richard left Max in the *haus* chewing on the wood and went to the barn to look for rope or something he could use as a makeshift collar and lead.

He hadn't looked closely in the barn before. There were leather straps and odds and ends that looked like they were a part of a harness. Richard strung some of the straps together and managed to make a collar and lead for Max.

Max was not impressed with the collar and lead and rolled in an effort to free himself. Once they were walking and on their way, Max forgot about the lead and bounded through the tall grass alongside him.

Richard had no idea where he was going, he just followed the direction that he saw Betsy head in, after she had kicked dirt at him and yelled at him. With visions of the angry woman in his head, he wondered if he was doing the right thing in going to see her.

What if she's still angry? Maybe she's like that all the time, he thought. Richard shrugged off his imaginings, after all he was trying to do the right thing and that's all he could do. If she did not accept his apologies, that would not his problem.

The closer Richard walked in Betsy's direction the more nervous he grew. He did not know how a woman could have that effect on him. After all he was a *mann* and had been a very successful *mann* in the *Englisch* world and was never intimidated or nervous of anybody.

Chapter 5

Be careful for nothing; but in every thing by prayer and supplication with thanksgiving let your requests be made known unto God.
And the peace of God, which passeth all understanding,
shall keep your hearts and minds through Christ Jesus.

Philipians 4:6-7

Betsy sat in her caravan. She had dressed and was ready to go out and find a job, but then she became filled with fear. Would just an ordinary job give her the large amount of money she needed? Maybe she should try and start up her own business again, like she had always wanted.

"Hello, is anyone there?"

Betsy was sure she heard a voice, but it was a voice that she did not recognize. She peeped out of the caravan's narrow window to see Richard

Black standing with a puppy in his arms. She opened the door and stepped out of the van. "Are you looking for me?"

Richard bent down to put Max on the ground then stood up, and said, "*Jah*, I've come to say I'm sorry."

Betsy looked at the pup. "That's a cute puppy."

"*Jah*, I got him yesterday."

"What's his name?" Betsy closed the distance of the five paces between them and patted the dog.

"Well, I've called him Max."

"Hello Max." She looked up at Richard and squinted a little as the morning sun was in her eyes. "Is he thirsty?"

"He could be. We've had a bit of a walk."

"I'll fetch him some water."

"*Denke*."

Betsy fetched her bottled water and poured some into a dish for Max. She stood up as Max lapped at the water. "How did you find me?"

"I just came in the general direction you disappeared to the other day." Richard's eyes were drawn to two fold up chairs. "Can we sit?"

Betsy nodded. "Jah."

Richard unfolded the two chairs. Betsy drew hers a little distance from where Richard had placed his so they wouldn't be too close to each other.

"So what are you sorry for?"

"Sorry for buying your house. I had no idea."

"You knew it was a foreclosure auction, so you knew the bank was foreclosing on someone. If no one bought it then they would've had to give me more time. They've tried to sell it before you know, and no one bought it."

Richard shook his head. "No, I didn't know that." Richard had bought a few properties over the years at foreclosure auctions, and never gave any thought to the people who were losing their homes. Now, it became very real to him as he sat with someone who had been forced out of their home. As he looked up at the old caravan, a pang of guilt ran through his body.

"Tell me something. When I entered the *haus* I could have sworn that nobody had lived there for quite some time. The only room that seemed lived in was the kitchen. Where did you sleep?"

"I slept and lived mostly in the little room off from the kitchen." Betsy shuddered. "I feel embarrassed for anyone to see the state of the place. I know it was nearly falling down around me, but I didn't know what to do. I only knew I couldn't give it up."

Richard raised his hand. "Wait a minute. There's a room off from the kitchen?"

Betsy nodded. "*Jah,* just next to the door of the utility room."

Richard laughed. "I saw the locked door and thought it was another cupboard." Richard tapped his chin. "So it's another room?"

Betsy nodded and moved uncomfortably in her chair.

"I've been searching for the key to that door, but haven't found one."

"Top shelf in the utility room – far right," Betsy said.

"Arr, thank you."

After a time of silence, Betsy said, "Sell it back to me then."

Richard drew his eyes away from hers and he remained silent.

"I used to work as a hat maker," Betsy continued.

His eyes fixed upon her as he wondered why she would all of a sudden talk of something else. He played along with her to see where her conversation would lead. "A milliner?"

"I guess you could say that."

"What type of hats did you make?"

"Men's hats mostly. Hats for the Mennonites, Amish and felt fedoras as well."

"Why aren't you doing that now?" Richard pressed his fingers together, in front of his chest.

"The store closed. I was working there seven days a week until they closed. I was trying to pay the bank the back-money I owed them."

"So that's why you didn't have enough money to keep the house in good repair?" Richard hoped that Betsy would not be offended by his questions, but she had acknowledged it was in bad repair.

"I guess so."

Richard studied her intently, and said, "Why didn't you let the community help you fix the *haus*?"

"I'd left off going to meetings frequently, and didn't want to bother anyone."

Richard begrudgingly admitted to himself that Betsy was beautiful, and under different circumstances he would be delighted in her company. "I suppose it was hard with you working all the time."

"*Jah*." She nodded and looked to the ground.

"Can you get another job making hats somewhere?"

"I was going to start a small workshop in the barn and make a little store out of the little cottage near the road. The cottage would've made an ideal store. The bank sold all the hat making machines and equipment that I had in the barn, even my hat blocks and then they sold the *haus*."

Betsy's story reminded him so much of what his friend, Abigail, had just been through. He knew that Abigail was under a tremendous amount of stress and Abigail had her *kinner* to lean on whereas this woman had no one. "Do you know why I bought the home?"

"I guess it was a *gut* investment or because it was inexpensive?"

"*Nee,* it was my old *familye* home. They built it over two hundred years ago, maybe closer to three."

Betsy's hands flew to her mouth as she gasped. "*Nee*. You're a Blough?"

"Yes, my grandmother, or should I say, *grossmammi* was Elizabeth Violetta Blough, and she ran away from home when she was sixteen to marry my grandfather who was an *Englischer.*"

"Was Elizabeth, Enid's *schweschder*?" Betsy's eyes had grown very wide.

"I'd say so, from what I've learned it sounds as though she must have been. I'm still doing research on the *familye*."

"So, Elizabeth must have never stayed in contact with her *familye*."

Richard shook his head. "I remember she told me she was Amish. She spoke of feeling restricted, of rules and regulations. She never spoke of the *gut* things that I've seen and experienced amongst the community.

Betsy shrugged and coldness invaded her eyes. "Maybe we want what we don't have."

Richard put his head to one side. "How do you mean? The grass is always greener, that type of thing?"

"You only see the things that you are missing out on, and not what you have – whatever they might be. Your *grossmammi* craved the things that were missing in her life, which sounds like it was freedom."

"I see what you mean. She was focused on not having certain liberties and possibly not looking at the things that she did have."

****

"Maybe." Betsy could feel her face soften into a smile. She had never found anyone who she could speak so freely with. Then she reminded herself that this was the *mann* who had stolen her *haus* from under her. She could not allow herself to be nice to this *mann.* Because of him she was living in the horrible cramped caravan. "Now that you have given your apologies for stealing my *haus*, what do you intend to do about it?"

****

Richard was amazed that she changed her tone so quickly. One minute she was chatting nicely, and the next minute she was speaking as if she had ice in her veins. "I didn't steal your *haus*."

"You did, and you even just said that you were sorry for doing so."

Richard jumped to his feet. His patience had worn thin. "Are you mad, woman?"

Betsy jumped to her feet also and took two steps forward to stare into his eyes. "How dare you say, that I'm mad. You get off my property right now, you and your little dog."

"You don't have a property, do you?" Richard laughed. "I'll leave your borrowed caravan on your borrowed property. Come on, Max."

"Why you …" Betsy picked up the nearest thing she could find which was the bowl that Max had been drinking out of. She threw it at Richard as he walked away. The bowl flew straight past his shoulder and he did not flinch, but kept on walking.

****

"The nerve of the man. He comes here to apologize then he denies any wrongdoing." Richard's words rang through her head, 'borrowed caravan' and 'borrowed land.' *Everything I have is borrowed, I don't own anything.* Betsy knew she should go out and look for a job, or she should plan on opening her own business, but today, it was all too much for her. She reclined on the bed, and even though it was mid morning, she went back to sleep.

****

As Richard walked away from Betsy, he was filled with regret over his hasty words. "Max, what came over me? Why didn't you stop me from saying those nasty things." Max kept rolling over as if he were tired, so Richard picked him up and carried him the rest of the way home.

Richard considered that the words that had just come out of his mouth were out of character for him. But this woman was like no other he had met. At one moment he was speaking to her freely and contentedly, and the next moment she was furious and not making any sense whatsoever.

I've ruined things, I've gone over to make amends and then I end up with a worse enemy than I had before. Why didn't I just keep my mouth shut? I said some horrid things to her, which only means that at some point I have to apologize again, he thought.

Richard knew that he had not made a good start to being Amish if he was letting this woman get under his skin. Maybe he needed to talk to the bishop about gaining patience.

He replayed the incident over in his mind, how quickly he reacted to her words in anger.

She was a woman going through a crises and he should have known better.

Once Richard was home, he located the key to the bedroom he'd just learned of from Betsy. The door opened onto a large room with a large brass bed as the feature. The bed was surely an antique and very fancy. Richard thought it a little too fancy to be in an Amis house, with its soft blue porcelain insets ,and curved pieces of brass.

Richard smiled as he looked around the room. It was truly a lady's room. It had a comfortable couch to sit on, side table, and handsome antique kerosene lamp. The room had a warm, homey feel to it. This explained how Betsy was able to live in the house at all, given the state of disrepair of the rest of it.

Richard sat on the bed and for the first time, he felt like an intruder in someone else's home.

Chapter 6

All scripture is given by inspiration of God, and is profitable for doctrine, for reproof, for correction, for instruction in righteousness:

2 Timothy 3:16

The next Sunday that the meeting was held, Betsy decided to attend. She needed some direction for her life, and direction could only come from *Gott.*

She went with her sister and her brother–in-law, since she no longer had a buggy or horse of her own. They arrived at the Millers' *haus* ten minutes before the meeting was due to start. Betsy hoped that she wouldn't see Richard because things were left so horribly between them.

Betsy had considered apologizing, but her heart wasn't ready. He had, after all, taken her *haus*. That was something that would take some time to get used to and just giving some trite apology hardly seemed appropriate.

Just as she was taking her seat, she spied Richard on the other side of the room. She begrudgingly admitted to herself that he did look handsome, and for some reason that made her feel worse for being mean to him.

Richard looked up, caught her eye and gave a smile and a little wave. Betsy looked behind her, as she was sure that the smile and the wave must have been meant for another. When she looked behind, she saw that there was no one. When she turned to face him, he had looked away.

Once the service was over, Betsy did not leave straight away. This time, she stayed for the meal because she had come with her *schweschder* and *bruder*-in-law. She had to learn a lot more about Richard Black if she was going to find a way to get him off her property.

She must try and turn people against him, but how? Perhaps, she could start a rumor. Before long she was with a group of women who began to speak of newest member of their community, Richard Black. Now was a perfect opportunity for her to muddy his name.

"They say, he's a *gut* catch," one of the women whispered.

"Look how tall and handsome he is," said another.

"I heard that he got an *Englischer* pregnant and he's hiding amongst the Amish so he won't have to pay a dime of child support." Betsy had made up the first thing that had come into her mind.

The women she was with gasped and shook their heads disapprovingly.

Betsy added, "I'm not sure if it's true, but it's what I've heard." The women gasped some more and as they did, Betsy felt ashamed that she would tell such blatant lies. Then again, it was all for the greater good. If he left the community she would have a chance at getting her house back.

Betsy hurried away from that group in case they asked questions, questions that she would not be able to answer.

Betsy found another group of women and joined in their conversation, all the time keeping an eye on Richard Black. He had been speaking to one of the ministers a few minutes before, and now he was speaking with Jakob Lapp.

When the meal was ready, Betsy walked toward the table with a couple of ladies.

She had lost sight of Richard Black. She scanned the crowed and then she saw him engaged in a conversation with Lucy Singer. Lucy was well known for being on the hunt for a husband – every one knew that. She was in her early twenties and was desperate to marry. To make matters worse, Richard looked delighted to be speaking with her.

Betsy considered that some might find Lucy attractive. She had olive brown skin, big brown eyes and black hair.

Betsy knew that if Richard and Lucy got married that would cement Richard into the community. *If he finds a fraa he will never leave the community, and I will never get my haus back.* She knew that she had to do something to stop a relationship between the two of them before one started.

"Ah Richard, there you are." Betsy stood very close to Richard and then turned her attention to Lucy. "Hello, Lucy. I see you've met my Richard."

Richard nearly choked. "Your Richard?"

Betsy laughed and stood even closer to him and slapped him playfully on his arm. "Too early to let people know, is it?"

Lucy looked disappointed and her eyes darted to Richard and then to the ground.

"What are you playing at, Betsy?" Richard asked.

"I had better go and get something to eat. It was nice to meet you, Richard." Lucy nodded her head to them both before she left.

Richard folded his arms in front of him, before he asked again, "Well, what are you playing at?"

Betsy wanted to walk away, but she was afraid if she left him alone he would be set upon by another single woman looking for a husband. There was only one thing she could do, she had to stay and talk with him a while longer. "That woman has a dubious reputation. I'm trying to protect you."

"She seemed lovely, and quite attractive too."

Betsy leaned forward and whispered, "Sometimes all is not what it seems."

Richard leaned close to her ear, and whispered back, "Maybe *you* are the one who is not what *you* seem."

Betsy giggled loudly so everyone might think that there was some fondness between them, and that would keep other women at bay. She had to keep the conversation going. "How's your dog?"

"Max is fine."

"How is your caravan?"

"Fine." Betsy wanted to stay longer and keep talking, for appearances sake only, but it was difficult to find conversation that would not develop into an argument.

"Betsy, I've been thinking."

Betsy looked up at him. He seemed as though he was going to say something serious. Maybe he was going to say that he would sell the house back to her. "*Jah*?"

"Perhaps we might be able to help each other."

She tipped her head to the side. The only way he could help her was to give her back her house.

Richard ignored her silence and continued, "What if you started up your hat business in my little cottage? That would help you, and that would help me by giving me rental income for the cottage."

Betsy knew he was trying to be nice, but it was hard to come to terms with having to pay rent for something that was once hers.

Betsy opened her mouth to speak, but Richard continued before she had a chance. "Meet me there tomorrow and we'll have a look at it together and go from there. What do you say?"

She nodded her head and walked away.

"About three o'clock?"

She turned to the sound of his voice and nodded. *How can he be so nice when I've been nothing but awful to him? I was trying to ruin his chances of finding a fraa and then he was nice to me. I must apologize to him tomorrow when I visit the cottage. My behavior has been bad,* she thought.

Chapter 7

In whom also we have obtained an inheritance, being predestinated according to the purpose of him who worketh all things after the counsel of his own will:

That we should be to the praise of his glory, who first trusted in Christ.

Ephesians 1:11-12

Richard spent a sleepless night wondering how he could help Betsy and allowing her use of the cottage seemed a perfect idea.

I think I'm making a breakthrough with her. I hope she likes me in a romantic way. She made Lucy think that we were together – a classic ploy to put the other woman off her game. Richard chuckled to himself. He had used that ploy himself in times past.

He did want a wife, but not one that came with thorns and briars such as Betsy. *Nee, she would be far too much for me to handle, especially when I want a quiet and peaceful life.* He hoped that they might have a friendship as neighbors do and nothing more.

****

At three o'clock the next day, they both arrived at the cottage.

Richard unlocked the door and Betsy walked through first.

"It's quite a decent size, isn't it," Richard said as he paced around the interior.

"*Jah*, and it's close to the road, which would make it ideal as a little store."

"Needs a few repairs; I'd say it could be ready in a few weeks. What are you thoughts?"

Betsy looked around once more, before she said, "It would be perfect."

"Would you be interested in leasing it?"

Betsy smiled at his kindness. "*Denke*, Richard. You've been so kind and I've been so horrible to you. I feel ashamed of myself and I must say that I'm sorry for how I've acted toward you."

"Apology accepted. It must be a stressful time for you."

Betsy nodded. *I have no money for stock, no money for machine,s and no money for rent,* she thought as she pondered what to say to him. Then she remembered that the bank owed her a small sum of money from the sale of the house.

She had to find out exactly what that amount was, and then she could make some plans. "I need to work out my finances. How much rent were you thinking?"

"Let's go back to the *haus* and we can work out some things."

Richard locked up the cabin, and they walked back together. Betsy's bad feelings towards him were being replaced by other feelings, which she was not familiar with. Were they feelings of fondness, or feelings of gratitude? Betsy admired Richard's 'take charge' attitude and forthrightness.

Maybe he's not as bad as I thought. But if I rent the cottage from him that just makes his position in my haus, and in the community, stronger. As they walked in silence, Betsy realized that renting the cottage from him was nothing to do with her original plan of forcing him out of the Amish community.

Maybe he knows what I was planning to do and he's trying to get me on side. He's a clever businessman after all – I'm sure he's trying to fool me.

Betsy hesitated outside her old home, and looked up at it.

"Let's go inside. I've got two chairs now." Richard laughed. "That's the only furniture I've got so far."

Betsy followed Richard through the door.

"Have a seat." Richard sat in one chair and waited for Betsy to sit in the other. "You've been quiet. Is running the hat business something that you want to do? If you do, it might help us both – you know?"

Betsy nodded. "*Jah*, I see what you mean. I'd need a work area to do the hats, there wouldn't be room enough in my caravan, and my *schweschder* doesn't have any room for such things in her small *haus.*"

"You could use the barn. I won't be using it 'til I get a horse and buggy, and even when I do there'd be more than enough room."

Betsy looked down into her hands that were folded in her lap. "Richard, why are you doing this? You could rent the cottage to anyone." Surely he wouldn't be devious enough to have worked out her plan of running him out of the community. How would he have figured it out? She looked into his face and waited for his response.

"Like I said, it would help both of us and maybe I do feel a little guilty for buying your *haus*. I had no idea what the bank had told you.

All I knew that it was a repossession – a foreclosure sale."

Betsy studied his face and considered him to be telling the truth.

"Betsy, I must say that I'd never given much thought to people affected by having their properties foreclosed upon. I've only ever seen things like that as an opportunity for someone to prosper from it. Of that, I'm deeply ashamed."

Her fingers fiddled nervously with the ends of her prayer *kapp;* he was sharing his flaws so openly. "It takes a lot to admit to something like that." *But you still have my haus and I'm living in a caravan*, she thought.

Betsy looked at the door as she heard scratching sounds.

"That's Max." Richard opened the door and let Max into the house. Max immediately ran to Betsy.

"Hello, Max." Max jumped up and licked Betsy.

"He likes you."

Betsy laughed as she tried to stop him from jumping excitedly. "He's a lovely dog."

"I never had much to do with dogs before. I only had a bunny when I was growing up."

Betsy laughed hard at the thought of Richard owning a bunny. "I'm sorry, it just seems funny. I can't imagine you with a bunny."

"I was very attached to him; just as I'm growing fond of Max. He's my best friend, and I've only had him a few days."

Betsy's mind was drawn back to more serious matters as she considered his offer of the cottage that she could turn into a store. If she made a lot of money in her business, her purpose would be to buy the property back.

How would she drive him out of the community and at the same time, rent the cottage from him? It would definitely muddy her plan of getting rid of him, if she took his offer.

"I'll have to give some serious thought to your offer. I thank you kindly for it."

"I'm very good at accounts, if you want to run some figures past me."

"*Denke,* but I don't know yet what the bank is giving me from the sale. It most likely won't be much."

"Well, once you can find that out perhaps we can talk again?"

He sat there smiling at her and she felt her heart race. *If only he wasn't an enemy, someone who ruined my life. I might find him a little appealing - if he was someone else,* she thought.

Richard leaned over and gave Max a good scratch on his belly. Betsy noticed that he looked adoringly at his dog.

"You really like that dog, don't you?"

"*Jah,* I truly do."

Maybe she was wrong about him – completely wrong. Someone who loved animals so much had to be a nice person. "Richard, I'm sorry for how rude I was to you the other day. I was upset, but that does not excuse how I behaved."

"You've already apologized. Don't give it another thought. I spoke rudely myself." He cleared his throat. "Let's start afresh." Richard put his hand out toward her and she put her hand in his and they shook. "I'm Richard Black."

Betsy laughed a little. "Pleased to meet you. I'm Betsy Baywell." Betsy felt a little better. It was much easier being friends with someone than being their enemy. Yet, she did not feel comfortable being a guest in a home that was once her own. "I should be getting home now." *Well, back to my caravan*, she thought as she rose to her feet.

Richard stood. "Must you go so soon?"

"*Jah*, I need to help my *schweschder* with something."

Richard walked out of the *haus* with her, and as she walked away she turned and said, "I'll be in touch."

"Soon, I hope."

****

Richard closed the front door, pleased that he had been nice to Betsy. *What a transformation, that woman is a real beauty when she isn't scowling. She's so easy to speak to and she has that little bit of a spark to her – I like that in a woman.*

He patted Max on the head. "You might be getting a new *mamm* soon." Richard laughed at his own words. *I'm jumping the gun, I know, but I could see myself with a woman such as Betsy, if she can get rid of her dark side.*

Chapter 8

Let your conversation be without covetousness; and be content with such things as ye have: for he hath said, I will never leave thee, nor forsake thee.

Hebrews 13:5

Richard was finally taking the plunge and buying his first horse. He was daunted about looking after such a large animal as a horse, but most of the Amish looked after horses, so he knew he would be able to get good advice.

Richard looked out of his front door and saw Jakob heading toward the *haus* from the road. "Right on time," he said out aloud. "Bye, Max you be a *gut* boy 'til I get home."

He climbed in the buggy next to Jakob.

"Are you ready for this?" Jakob asked.

"Well, I've got the stable in the barn ready like you told me. I've got a brand new buggy just waiting. So all we need is a great looking horse."

Jakob laughed. "There's nothing to it."

Richard screwed up his face. He would much rather get in a car, push a button and drive. It seemed a lot of fiddling around having to hitch and unhitch a buggy, and make sure all the equipment was in working order. Then there was the horse, feeding it and tending to his or her needs. *Jah, a car is so much easier*, he thought.

He would have transport rather than having to take a taxi everywhere. A buggy was some sort of independence.

"I'm glad you know about horses, because I know nothing," Richard said.

"You soon will. I'll get a *gut* one for you, don't worry."

They walked through the rows of horses for sale, while Richard tried not to worry about the horse droppings getting on his new boots. Richard had no idea what he was looking for, but was drawn to a black horse with a white blaze that covered most of his face. "Jakob, what about that one over there?"

"That one's a Standardbred. Let's have a closer look."

Richard stood next to Jakob as he read the summary of the horse's details.

"This one is eight years old, not too young, or too old." Jakob pulled the horse's mouth opened and looked at his teeth. "Do you like this one?"

"*Jah*, I do. Would he be all right? He looks like he could pull a buggy."

"Let's see, he's number eleven, so we'll bid on him, and the bay over there, number fifteen – that is, if this one goes too high."

Richard screwed up his face. He'd have that horse no matter what the price.

The auction began, and Jakob and Richard took a position where the auctioneer could see them clearly.

As the hammer fell on the second horse, Richard sensed someone beside him. He turned to see Lucy. "Hello, Lucy."

Lucy smiled up at him. "You buying a horse?"

"*Jah*. What brings you here?"

"My *bruder* works here, and *mamm* sent me here because he forgot to take his lunch with him today."

"Hello, Lucy." Jakob leaned across Richard to speak. "Your horse's coming up soon, Richard."

"Excuse me, Lucy. I must concentrate on this." Richard turned his back on Lucy to concentrate on the auction. He did not want to miss out on his black horse.

Lucy stood beside him quietly while Richard won the bidding.

"Congratulations, Richard," Lucy said.

Richard turned around to speak to her and was quite surprised to see that she was standing so close to him. "*Denke*, Lucy."

"Is he broken to harness?"

"I hope so. According to Jakob he is."

"I must come around when you try him out for the first time," Lucy said.

Richard smiled at Lucy while trying to figure out how to politely decline the invitation she had just given herself. "Well, I'm not exactly sure when that will be, and I'm quite busy over the next few weeks."

"I can have him to your place by tonight, and we can harness him up tomorrow," Jakob said.

Richard pressed his lips together firmly as he shot Jakob a disapproving look, for opening his mouth.

"I'm free tomorrow. I'll come out to see how he goes." Lucy nodded to both men before she left.

"What have you done, Jakob? I'm not really ready for visitors; I've not even settled in myself."

Jakob slapped him on the back. "Just trying to help. Abigail said you were looking for a *fraa* and you could do worse that Lucy."

"*Denke*, Jakob, but she's hardly my type."

Jakob rubbed his *baard.* "I'm sorry. I thought the two of you seemed to be getting along. I was trying to help things along."

"I might be new to the Amish, but I'm not new to the dating world. I'm more than capable of choosing my own *fraa*." Richard's brow furrowed.

"Lucy's a fine looking woman, and seems to be fond of you."

Richard wondered if that was the problem. Lucy was far too eager to please, and there seemed to be no depth to her. He wanted someone he could talk to and someone who would not agree with everything he said – someone who could think for herself, and have her own opinions.

Jakob grunted, and said, "Let's go and pay for this horse."

****

Jakob was there the next day as he said he would be. They hitched up Richard's brand new buggy to the horse. The horse was the perfect buggy horse and handled beautifully.

"You've got a mighty fine horse there. He doesn't flinch at anything and he's quick on the uptake – seems to know what you want before you ask him." Jakob got out of the buggy and handed the reins to Richard.

"I hope he does the same for me." Richard took hold of the thick leather reins.

"Just walk up the driveway, turn around and trot back to me."

Richard did just that. He remembered all that he had learned from the Fishers and the horse went perfectly. As he pulled up, from a trot in front of Jakob, he said, "I think I could get used to this."

"*Gut*." Jakob chuckled loudly. "Do you want to go out on the road?"

"Just a little ways to start with. You'll have to come with me to check that I'm doing everything right."

Jakob jumped in and they drove the buggy up and down the road outside of Richard's property.

Richard had neither seen nor heard from Lucy, and he hoped she had forgotten she said she'd visit.

It wasn't 'till Jakob was leaving that Lucy showed up.

Jakob past Lucy's buggy in Richard's driveway. Richard put his hands on his head briefly then looked up with a smile so Lucy would not see the truth of his feelings.

"Hello, Lucy. I'm afraid you've missed it all. We tried the horse out, now we've put him away," Richard walked up to her buggy door, hoping she would say she would not stay.

"Never mind. I've got a little time before I have to get back home." She stepped down. "Show me around."

There was nothing he could do. He was trapped. Trapped into being polite and showing Lucy around his *haus.*

"There's not much to see. It hasn't been renovated yet. It's quite a mess."

Lucy walked through the front door. "Oh my. It certainly needs a woman's touch." As she entered the kitchen she turned around to Richard, and said, "Who cooks for you?"

Richard knew what was coming next. If he said no one cooked for him she might offer to come and cook for him. At that moment, Richard and Lucy heard a noise coming from the back of the house.

****

Betsy was going for a walk in the warm, summer sun when she found herself near

Richard's place. Once she saw Lucy's buggy, she had to have a peak in the window to see what was going on. The last thing she wanted was for Richard to be keen on an Amish woman, and for the woman to reciprocate those feelings. Then he'd never leave the Amish.

The window was just a little too high for her to peak through, so she picked up a wooden storage box nearby and stood on it. The box was rotted and she fell straight through it, just as she had caught sight of both Richard and Lucy. A yell escaped her lips. She tried to free herself from the rotting wood, but it was too late. She looked up to see that Richard had suddenly appeared around the corner of the house, quickly followed by Lucy.

Richard stood with his arms folded in front of his chest.

Betsy had to think quickly. "Hello, I was just trying to clean the windows for you."

"That was very nice of you, Betsy, but I thought you were going to do the windows for me tomorrow."

Betsy did not know if she was hearing correctly. Was he actually playing along with her lies?

Richard turned to Lucy. "Betsy does my cleaning and she also does my cooking, to answer your earlier question."

Lucy looked at Betsy with a downturned mouth. "Oh."

Betsy was still trapped by the rotting wood and was trying to free herself. "I'd appreciate a hand."

Richard stepped toward her and offered his strong arm. Betsy took hold and he pulled her free from the timber boards of the old box. He held onto her hands and looked down into her eyes. It was a moment that courting couples might have, but never in front of another.

"I should go," Lucy said, from behind them.

"We'd love to have you stay, Lucy. I could make you some *kaffe,"* Betsy freed herself from Richard's grasp and stepped back. Breathing in Richard's scent made Betsy's heart beat too quickly.

"*Denke*, Betsy, but I promised *mamm* I'd be home early."

Betsy nodded and both Betsy and Richard followed Lucy out to her buggy. They both waved Lucy goodbye as if they were a courting couple. When she was out of sight, Richard turned to Betsy. "*Denke* for saving me."

Betsy smiled up at him, pleased that he was not interested in Lucy.

"Now, you can tell me what you were doing spying on me."

Betsy bit her lip. What reason could she possibly give? "I was just out walking in the sunshine and wondered if Max wanted to go for a little walk with me. I didn't want to disturb you, and I wondered if he was in the house with you." Betsy looked up at him from under her lashes to see if he was being fooled by her tale. “Where is he anyway?”

“I shut him in one of the stables while I was trying my new horse and new buggy.”

Betsy’s shoulders drooped. He had gone out and bought a horse and a buggy, which was a sign that he wasn’t tired of the Amish life.

“Why so glum?”

She shook her head. “Nothing.”

“Come with me, and I’ll let Max out of the stable.”

Betsy dawdled behind him as he strode toward the stable. They both peeked into the stable to see that Max was fast asleep on an old blanket.

“He looks so cute,” Betsy said.

“*Jah*, I think I’ll leave him sleep for a while. I’ll open the door so he can come out when he finishes his nap.”

When they walked out of the barn, Betsy said, “You were pretending that we were a couple in front of Lucy.”

Richard stood still and threw his hand on his heart dramatically. “What do you mean?”

Betsy laughed. “Just then, when Lucy was here. You wanted her to think that I was your girl, and don’t deny it.”

Richard smiled and leaned his arm on the wall of the barn. “I think she’s taken a fancy to me.”

What woman wouldn’t is what Betsy thought, but she said, “And you don’t find her appealing?”

“She’s not the woman for me.”

Betsy folded her arms and tipped her head sideways. “And what type of woman would be for you?”

“Someone with a spark. Someone who speaks their mind, and has an opinion of their own. Someone with light brown hair with streaks of gold.”

Betsy instinctively touched her own hair that peeped out from her prayer *kapp.* He was describing her hair. “Sounds like you’ve given quite some thought to this." She quickly put her hand to her side as she became aware of what she was doing.

Richard laughed and took his arm away from the wall. "Not really, I don't see myself with anyone."

Betsy nodded and quickly said, "That's best." She was not about to encourage him to find a *fraa.* Things were bad enough now that he'd bought himself a horse and buggy; a *fraa* would be the worst thing. At least he could sell the horse and buggy when he gave up on the idea of being Amish, but a *fraa* was a lifetime commitment.

"And what about you, Betsy? Ever think about marriage?"

"If it's *Gott's* will it'll happen. I've no need for it."

Richard and Betsy looked into each other's eyes for a moment before Betsy looked away. Her mouth had suddenly become dry as she had an overwhelming desire to be held in his strong arms, and press her body into the hardness of his.

What was happening to her? She had to get far away from him immediately. “I must go.” She walked past Richard. He caught her gently by her arm and pulled her into him.

Instantly was in front of her, their bodies pressed together. She looked up into his eyes and they burned into hers with a hunger that she’d never known. His arm was firmly around her waist, the other holding her hand. He lowered his lips slowly until they gently touched hers.

“*Nee.*” She pulled away from him and ran. She ran past his house, through the fields and all the way back to the safety of her caravan.

Betsy breathlessly threw herself on the bed and pressed one hand on her beating heart. That was the first time she had allowed a *mann* to be so close. She touched her lips gently with her fingers, while she remembered his scent and the touch of his warm, soft lips upon hers.

****

Richard's body trembled all over, his legs gave way and he sank to the ground. He licked his lips and they tasted of her – they tasted of honey and flowers - of Betsy.

She made his heart race like no other woman had. *Could this be the woman for me? Or have I been alone for so long that any woman looks good? Maybe my mind is playing tricks on me.* He remembered their first meeting when she accused him of stealing his property. She was not the stable, normal woman he imagined he would share his life with. *Why is it that I find a woman like that so intoxicating?*

Chapter 9

And God said, Let us make man in our image, after our likeness: and let them have dominion over the fish of the sea, and over the fowl of the air, and over the cattle, and over all the earth, and over every creeping thing that creepeth upon the earth.

Genesis 1:26

Two days later, Betsy saw Max near her caravan. She looked around for Richard, but he was nowhere to be seen.

"Max, here boy." Max ran to Betsy and she carried him into the caravan and found some strong yarn.

"What are you doing all the way out here? You know I'm going to have to take you back now, don't you?" Betsy looped the yarn through Max's collar and attached it to the front of her van.

She patted Max on his head while trying to avoid his licks. "You stay here while I get dressed. I can't let anyone see me like this." Thoughts of the other day had haunted Betsy's mind almost every second.

She wondered how things would be between them, when she saw him again. Now she had an excuse to see him; she had to take Max back to him.

Betsy only had her nightdress on so she pulled it off and reached for her dress. As she changed, she heard an angry voice.

"What in the world?"

Betsy knew that voice belonged to Richard Black. She dressed quickly and opened the caravan door. There was no time to brush her hair, let alone put her prayer *kapp* on.

Richard was bent over Max untying him. As he looked up, he said, "So you're a dog stealer now? It's not enough that you've accused me of stealing, and you've tried to turn everyone against me." He stood glaring at Betsy with the end of the yarn in his hand and the other end attached to Max's collar.

"*Nee*, you have the whole thing wrong. I just found him. I was on my way to get him back to you."

"You were in your van. Doesn't look like you're planning to go anywhere." She put her hand to her hair, suddenly self conscious of her untidiness. "I was in my nightdress, and I found him and tied him up. I couldn't take him back in my night dress, could I?" Betsy found confidence from somewhere as she leaned against the van door and gave him a challenging stare. "Or would you have liked that?"

"Just when I was starting to think you were a decent person. You're nothing but a …" Richard looked at her for a moment before he turned and walked away without finishing what he was saying. Max walked dutifully by his side. After a few paces he turned around to see Betsy still looking at him. "You're nothing but a horrible person, the likes of which I have never met before, and I've come across some terrible people."

"Richard you have things wrong." She stepped down from her caravan.

"The only thing wrong I have is that I thought that we might be friends. Two days ago I even thought we could be more than friends. Now I see that I was wrong about that. I was even going to help you get your hat machines back."

Betsy put her hand to her throat. It seemed hopeless, nothing she could say now would make him believe that the dog ran away and she did not steal him.

Maybe she was wrong about him. Maybe he was a horrible person if he preferred to believe his own delusions. "That's right I stole your little dog. I'm so hungry I was going to roast him for lunch, since I'm too poor to buy any food." Betsy picked up the nearest thing, which was a tin cup and threw it at Richard.

The cup hit Richard on the shoulder. He looked at her for a moment before he walked away in silence, shaking his head.

Betsy closed the van door very loudly to be sure that Richard could hear the slam. *If that's what happens when I try to do him a favor, then I won't ever do it again.* Betsy fought back tears, it seemed as if nothing was going right for her at all. She was even starting to like the stranger who had stolen her *haus,* until he jumped to the wrong conclusions as if she were a common thief.

Betsy did not want to get dressed at all. All she wanted to do was go back to sleep and hope that her life had just been one long, bad dream. Maybe she would wake up and find that she had found a *gut mann* to marry and had six *kinner* who were all perfectly polite and well-behaved. Maybe she would wake up and she would still have her *haus,* the bank having given her more time to pay. *I might as well know now that this is my life, no gut trying to make it something it's not. I have to make the best of it.*

****

Richard's heart thumped hard. He did not know whether it was from having a tin cup thrown at him and being yelled at, or could it have been because he found the sight of Betsy's long hair cascading about her, breathtaking?

"Did you see her Max? Did you see how beautiful she looked standing at the door with her hair like that?" Max didn't reply or even look up at Richard.

She could be a fashion model if it weren't for that angry, sullen face of hers. It doesn't matter what she looks like if she's crazy. What type of crazy woman would steal someone's dog?

Why is it that the most beautiful women never have a beautiful mind or heart to go with it? Maybe I should ask Lucy on a date to take my mind off Betsy. Lucy seems a little dull, but dull might be a welcome change to crazy, Richard thought.

Chapter 10

Therefore if any man be in Christ, he is a new creature:

old things are passed away; behold,

all things are become new.

2 Corinthians 5:17

Determined to push the crazy dog-stealing Betsy Baywell out of his mind, Richard asked Lucy out to dinner. *Maybe I haven't given Lucy a fair chance; maybe there is something more to her than I've seen,* he thought.

It was at a barn raising when Richard had an opportunity to speak to Lucy next. She'd just arrived when he approached her.

"Lucy, will you have dinner with me some time?"

Lucy smiled and said, "Aren't you and Betsy courting?"

"*Nee*, we aren't." Richard looked to the

ground, ashamed of his behavior the day Lucy had visited him.

"It seemed like that the other day. She does all your cooking and cleaning for you, doesn't she?"

Richard laughed. "*Nee*, she's just my neighbor."

"Nothing more?" Lucy gazed up at him with huge round eyes.

Richard shifted his weight from one leg to the other. Asking an Amish woman out was proving more difficult than he thought it would be. "Nothing more."

"Then I'd love to have dinner with you?"

"Monday night then?"

Lucy nodded. "*Jah* that would be fine."

Richard arranged to fetch Lucy at her house then they would go to a local restaurant.

Richard had never done manual labor before, so he considered he wouldn't be much use at all with the barn raising. He did a few jobs that didn't require much skill and stayed until late doing all that he could. It felt good to be part of a community that helped each other.

* * *

On Monday night, Richard took Lucy to the restaurant, as arranged.

While they were eating, Lucy said, "I've heard some things about you."

"I'm sure you have, but if they're bad you can be sure that they aren't true."

"Hmm, I thought as much. It appears someone is spreading stories about you."

"It's quite likely." Richard had already heard a little of the stories and rumors that surrounded him, but he didn't want to waste time with Lucy speaking of them. "Now tell me about yourself, Lucy."

Lucy did not waste any time to do so. "I'm twenty two, I can cook well and sew and love looking after children. I can't wait to have my own *kinner.*" Lucy smiled broadly at Richard before she paused to have another sip of soda.

Richard considered Lucy to be very forward, she was throwing herself at him, but still that may be the Amish way – he wasn't sure. "I see, and what else do you like to do?"

"I like to cook and sew, that keeps me busy."

"Do you have any goals? Would you ever like to have a job?"

Lucy giggled loudly and Richard hoped that the people in the restaurant would not think that they were a couple. He suddenly wanted to be anywhere other than where he was right now.

"*Nee*, I don't want a job. I want to get married and have lots of *kinner*." Lucy giggled, blushed a little, and again, looked adoringly into Richard's eyes.

After Richard took Lucy back to her home, he knew that she definitely was not the woman for him. Hopefully one day he would find a nice normal Amish woman who wasn't crazy or angry and who didn't have an annoying laugh. There was just something about a woman being too eager that put him off.

Richard unhitched the buggy, rubbed the horse down as Jakob had shown him, and walked back into his house.

He groaned as he opened the door. "I'm way too old for this." The buggy was not like owning a car where you could just stop it, lock it and forget it – a buggy and horse were hard work. On top of that, he had to come home to a dusty wreck of a place with two chairs and a sleeping bag as his only comforts. He could have stayed in the room Betsy used to sleep in, but he would feel he was intruding in her space.

He made up his mind then and there to get cracking along with the renovations.

****

With Betsy's latest argument with Richard Black, she knew the offer to rent the cottage for her business would be off the table. She was back to square one with no idea what to do. She would have to go into town and try and find a job – any kind of job.

Betsy borrowed Grace's buggy and headed into town. She went to every business that was run by Amish folk. She considered that was her best chance of employment.

The last place she came to was a haberdashery store. Betsy was a regular customer of the store so she knew the two ladies who ran it. They informed her that they were about to place an advertisement for an extra person. With Betsy's hat making experience, she got the job on the spot.

"*Denke, Gott.*" Betsy silently sent thanks to *Gott*, she knew that getting a job so quickly could only have come from Him. The store was owned and run by two elderly spinsters who were also sisters their names were, Milly and Vida Hilty. They were from the same community as Betsy and she knew she would like working with them.

While Betsy was driving the buggy back home to Grace's place, she was pleased that she would be working six days of every week and she would not have time to think of Richard Black. In fact she would put Richard Black and the harm he'd done to her, right out of her mind. She knew in her heart that she would get her *haus* back one day.

****

Richard was fuming about Betsy stealing his dog and fuming about her making up nasty rumors about him. He was trying his best to fit into the Amish lifestyle and it appeared that she was trying to block him at every turn. He was so upset that he made an appointment to discuss things with the bishop. He would of course, have to do so without naming Betsy as the person spreading foul rumors.

"Wie gehts, Richard," the bishop said as he greeted him in his drive-way.

Once they were sitting inside, face to face across the table, Richard said, "I'm harboring feelings of anger and I don't know how best to get rid of the feelings."

The bishop put his hand up to his dark *baard* and stroked it twice. "Hmm, and are these feelings toward a particular person?"

Richard searched his mind to recall if he was angry with anyone other than Betsy. "*Nee*, it's only one person."

"*Jah*, that's what I asked, if it was toward one person."

Richard nodded; there was a little communication problem, as the bishop spoke quite quickly. Richard could not determine what was Pennsylvania Dutch and what was English. He hoped that other people came to the bishop to discuss things as he was about to otherwise he was going to look a right fool.

"Would this person be female?" A smile spread across the bishop's face and a twinkle came to his eye.

"*Jah*, it is a female." Richard wondered if the bishop had heard that Betsy was spreading rumors about him.

The bishop leaned in close to Richard and

beckoned Richard to lean in as well. "That's how things started with, Mary. No matter what she did it made me cranky – almost crazy. I couldn't stand the woman when I first met her."

Richard whispered, "Mary, your *fraa*?"

The bishop laughed quietly. "*Jah*, maybe you should marry this girl who makes you cranky." He scratched his *baard.* "I can tell you Richard the happiest times of my life have been with Mary."

Richard put his two hands to his head. Was this really any kind of advice – and coming from a bishop? Richard straightened in his chair and put his hands by his sides. "*Nee*, it's nothing like that. Nothing like that at all."

The bishop just looked at him and one eyebrow raised, just slightly.

"You see this woman is the most objectionable, stubborn…" Richard could not finish his sentence or he would have had to say, intoxicating, annoyingly beautiful and the most captivating woman he had ever come across.

Richard lowered his head and said quietly, "I'm in trouble."

The bishop laughed while his wife, Mary, fussed about them offering nettle tea, sugar cookies and cake.

Richard left the bishop's *haus* shaking his head. *It's clear the bishop thinks I'm in love with Betsy. That's ridiculous, but why do I crave her company? I am drawn to learn more about her.* Richard touched his lips as he remembered the embrace he had with Betsy and the sensations that invaded his body when their lips touched, so softly.

Chapter 11

Now unto him that is able to do exceeding
abundantly above all that we ask or think,
according to the power that worketh in us,
Unto him be glory in the church by Christ Jesus
throughout all ages,
world without end. Amen.
Ephesians 3:20-21

Betsy sat on the floor of her caravan and cried, "*What am I to do, Gott? Please help me out of this mess I am in.*"

Betsy knew that *Gott* would only get her out of the mess she was in if she confessed her sin; her sin of spreading rumors about Richard Black. It was a horrible thing to do and she wanted to hurt him, but now she was the one who was hurting.

I will have to tell the bishop what I've done. I hope he does not have me confess in front of the whole community on a Sunday – I shall die of embarrassment. I will confess to the bishop, but not today.

Today was Betsy's first day at her new job and she was determined to make a *gut* impression on the two elderly ladies she worked for. She had Grace take her to work so she would arrive half an hour early.

As they started, Grace clicked the horse forward, and said, "Do you think that you will like working there?"

"I guess so. The ladies seem very nice. They're a little bit funny how they speak to each other. They have little nit-picking arguments between themselves."

"Grace, can we drive up this way? I want to go passed my old *haus,* well passed the road not passed the *haus* itself."

Grace turned and studied Betsy's face. "You're not spying on him, are you?"

"*Nee*, of course not." Betsy straightened her prayer *kapp,* as she looked at her *haus* surrounded by clouds of white dust. "I wonder what is happening?"

"Shall we go and see?"

"*Nee*, of course not. Anyway, I'll be late for work if we do."

"We've got plenty of time."

"*Nee*, Grace, just keep driving."

As Grace drove passed, Betsy turned around to see if she could get a better look at what was happening to her *haus.*

Once they were some distance up the road, Grace said, "Well, did you see him then?"

"Grace, stop it. I wasn't looking for that terrible *mann*. I was just seeing what he was doing to my *haus."* Betsy bit on her lip and waited for her *schweschder* to correct her and tell her that it wasn't her *haus* any longer – thankfully she didn't.

Betsy pushed the door of the Haberdashery store open and her two bosses; Milly and Vida met her at the door.

"Welcome to you, dear," Milly said.

Milly seemed to be the older of the two ladies. She was certainly the bossiest and the one to make all the decisions. The old ladies were similar to look at, they both had white hair like wool, shoulders slightly stooped, and were stick thin.

"Vida, you show Betsy where everything is, and I'll sort out some jobs that Betsy can do between serving customers."

"Very well, Milly." Vida tucked her arm through Betsy's. "Come this way."

Vida showed Betsy where everything was, as she was instructed. Once she was done showing her around, Vida said, "It wonders me that you're not married, Betty."

Betsy giggled. "It's Betsy actually."

"Forgive me, Betsy." Vida stared vacantly at the ceiling, as she said, "I had a very dear friend once, named Betty." Vida paused and took a slow breath. "She got very ill and eventually she died, but she was a very *gut* friend to me when she was alive, before she got sick." Vida turned her attention back to Betsy.

Betsy wasn't sure what to say to the old lady who was staring intently into her eyes. "It's nice to have a *gut* friend. If you aren't married, you only have friends, don't you?"

Betsy was not sure where this conversation was going, but the dear old lady meant no harm with her useless prattle. "*Jah*, I suppose so."

"Much chance of you getting a husband do you think - before you get much older?"

Betsy stifled a gasp at the old lady's enquiry.

Milly stepped in between them. "Vida, leave Betsy alone."

Milly pulled Betsy aside. "Come over here, Betsy. You sew don't you?"

"*Jah*, of course I can sew anything that you'd like me to sew."

"We've got an order for curtains. Do you think you could do that?"

"*Jah*, curtains are easy. Really, it's sewing a straight line."

"*Gut*, there are the measurements and it's that roll of gold brocade fabric over there." Milly stepped in closely and said in a low voice. "Forgive my *schweschder,* she forgets her manners sometimes."

"It didn't bother me at all." The truth was it did bother her a little, of course, there was little chance of her getting a husband at her age.

"She's a silly old lady sometimes," Milly said.

Betsy considered it best to make no reply and put her head down to study the measurements for the curtains.

"The cutting table is over there and the fabric scissors are in the drawer." Vida called to her from the other side of the room. "Remember, measure twice and cut once."

"I will, *denke*."

"I'm sure she knows what she's doing, Vida." Milly's tone was sharp.

Time must have flown by because it was no time at all when Vida said, "It's lunch time, Betty. You can have a break now."

"Okay, *denke*."

"Your break is half an hour and no longer, Betty," Vida said.

Betsy wondered if she should correct Vida once more over her name, but considered it probably didn't really matter if she called her Betty.

Vida walked slowly over to where Betsy sat. "Did you bring some lunch with you? You can share my pea soup if you didn't."

"Oh *denke*, but I did bring my own."

"You can eat out the back there, we don't like anyone eating near the fabrics."

"I understand." Betsy folded the fabric neatly and left it next to the machine and headed out to the backroom to eat her lunch. To her surprise, Vida followed her and sat next to her.

"Wonders me why a pretty girl like you isn't married."

Betsy could barely contain her laughter at the elderly lady repeating herself and talking again, of marriage. Betsy only hoped that she would not talk about marriage the whole time she was eating lunch.

Her *schweschder*, Milly, called out, "You've said that to her already, Vida. Just leave her alone and let her eat."

"Don't you tell me what to do. I own half of this place; you can't tell me what to do. Anyway, we're both eating lunch now, so it's not your business whatever I say." Vida leaned over to Betsy and put up her hand against her cheek as if she were telling a secret. "I didn't say that before, did I?"

Betsy half shrugged her shoulders and attempted a little shake of her head. She did not want to get caught between the two ladies arguing.

Vida whispered, "She thinks she owns this place, but she doesn't, I own half."

"I can hear what you're saying, Vida." Milly's voice rang loud and clear from the store.

"Hmmph." Vida opened up a plastic container of soup, took a spoon from the drawer and began to eat the cold soup.

Betsy was pleased she hadn't accepted her offer to share, what turned out to be *cold* pea soup. She had to stop herself laughing at Vida loudly slurping her soup from the spoon.

"How long have you owned this place?"

Vida looked up from her soup. "We've had this place for nearly forty years. I was just a young girl when we opened this place."

"*Nee*, you were old. We were both old when we opened this place and now we're both a lot older." Milly's voice again, was projected from the store and Betsy could only assume there were no customers who might be able to overhear the chatter.

Betsy believed the two ladies might be in their seventies or possibly their early eighties. They certainly looked very old to be running a business. She wondered if she might be old one day and running a business as a spinster, just like one of these ladies. Not that it would be a bad thing, if that were to be her lot in life - they did seem to enjoy themselves.

Once Betsy had finished eating, she went back to the showroom to the little area where the sewing machine was set up.

Milly came over to her and inspected her work. "That's a marvelous job. We didn't really employ you to do sewing. It's just that our regular girl who sews for us is away. This curtain order is due in the next couple of days. Do you mind if we get you to fill in with the sewing now and again?"

"I truly don't mind at all." Betsy didn't mind what she did, in fact the busier she was, the better. "What will be my regular duties?"

"Just sales mostly. Selling to people who walk in, and advising them on fabric choices, that kind of thing." Milly sat on the table and looked at Betsy in the chair. "You said the other day that you used to make hats?"

"*Jah*, I worked at Thomas' Hatmakers until they closed down."

Milly nodded. "I know Thomas' Hatmakers quite well. Why did they close?"

"I'm not really sure why they closed. It was quite sudden, that's all I know."

Milly rubbed her chin with the back of her hand. "Were they busy?"

"I was kept busy enough making the hats. I was never sitting around with nothing to do, but not all the hats were special orders. I did make a lot for the store as stock."

"I've had it in my mind for a time to make a little side business here with hats. I'm just mulling it over at this stage. I bought some equipment in a sale recently, so I'll guess that'll come in handy if I go ahead with it."

Betsy just nodded and said nothing. Could it be that she bought her hat making machines that the bank took from her? Betsy was far too embarrassed to ask such a personal question as where Milly had bought the machines. If they did turn out to be her machines what then? Surely that would make Milly feel awkward for having bought the machines. Jah, best she keep quiet about such things.

"If you do decide to, then I would be happy to make the hats."

Milly nodded her head and said, "*Gut*," and looked thoughtful as she walked away.

It was then that a thought occurred to Betsy, if Milly did not go ahead with the hat making, maybe she could buy the equipment back. Surely the second hand equipment would be much less a cost than brand new equipment.

"Remember, Betty cut once and measure twice." Vida's voice reverberated around the store as she yelled out from the back room and even Milly had to laugh.

Betsy caught Milly's eye from across the room and Milly mouthed the words, 'I'm sorry' to her, which made Betsy have to stifle a giggle.

When the store closed for the day, Betsy realized that she'd laughed more in one day than she had laughed in an entire month.

Chapter 12

That Christ may dwell in your hearts by faith;

that ye,

being rooted and grounded in love,

Ephesians 3:17

Richard woke up in good spirits; it was a beautiful sunny day. He walked outside the *haus* with Max, and looked up at it. Today he had the builders in and they were redoing the walls and replacing some of the rotting floorboards.

The house had been grand at one point in time. Not grand in a decorative kind of way, but grand in the way that it was large and stately. It was large enough to be converted to a B&B. Although that was not what Richard had in mind, he wanted a quiet and peaceful life. He need not have bought such a grand home and certainly would have bought a smaller house, if it weren't for the fact that this home had been built by his ancestors.

From his research, he found that the Bloughs had built the house and it was one of the area's oldest homes. The home consisted of an unusual central stone chimney, and a kitchen that had to be built by a skilled master craftsman. The cabinetry in the kitchen had stood the test of time and was remarkably still in excellent working order. The floors throughout were made from wide planks of a wood that Richard was unfamiliar with, but would certainly find out what they were. Many of the boards were in good condition.

The central point in the kitchen was a huge, blue-stone walk in fireplace with cast iron stove.

The third floor had been used at some stage as a fourth bedroom, but was most likely used as an attic one point in time. From this room, the wooden rafters and the high roof line could be admired. All the bedrooms were facing over the property.

Richard did not know what the cottage would have been used for and thought that maybe, it was for the older folk of the family or for other relatives.

Richard was suddenly aware of the clip-clop of hooves and looked around to see Abigail approaching his house in her buggy.

He walked over to her and helped her out. "Abigail, what brings you here today?" Richard looked at Abigail's clean clothes then back to the dust coming from the *haus*. "I'm pleased to see you, of course."

"I've been saying I'll come and have a look at the place."

Richard looked over his shoulder at the clouds of dust billowing from the door and the windows. "I'm afraid there's not much to see today. I'm having the walls pulled down so they can put new surfaces on the walls, some of the boards replaced, and a few other things."

"Well, I do have a tiny ulterior motive," Abigail said, as she smoothed down her dress with her hands.

Richard laughed. "Come over here away from the dust." Richard guided Abigail by the arm, towards the barn.

"I'm inviting you to dinner tomorrow night."

Richard raised one dark eyebrow. "Is this a match making dinner?"

Abigail laughed. "How could you know that?"

"I knew it was more than just a casual invitation." Richard wondered if he could ever find a woman as nice as Abigail. If only things were different and she had chosen him instead of Jakob. Of course, it was useless between the two of them now that she was married to Jakob.

"*Jah*, I do have a woman coming. She's very nice and I think you will be pleasantly surprised."

Richard's gaze fell on the horizon, which was bright against the morning sunlight. What could it hurt to have dinner at Abigail and

Jakob's *haus?* If he did not get along with the new woman he could always talk to Abigail or Jakob. "Fine, I'll be there."

"Are you sure that you can stay in the *haus* while all this is happening? You are welcome to stay with us while you're renovating."

"*Denke* for your offer. Max and I have made a little place for ourselves in the barn for the next couple of nights. Then, after that, we'll go back into the *haus*."

"Be sure to bring Max over and he can play with the other dogs."

"Okay, I'll do that."

"I'll see you tomorrow night then. Don't forget." Abigail climbed back into her buggy.

"I won't," Richard called after her.

****

Betsy could wait no longer. It played on her heart that she had spread evil rumors about another person. She arrived at the bishop's house without even making an appointment to see him.

The bishop ushered her into his house.

"I've done a terrible thing," she said as soon as she sat.

The bishop sat opposite her at his kitchen table. "Go on."

"I've told people untrue things about Richard Black."

The bishop did not look shocked, as she had expected he would. "What kind of things?"

Betsy put her face up to the ceiling and blew out a deep breath. It was too horrible to speak of and it was especially too horrible to tell the bishop, but she had to. "I told people that Richard Black fathered a child and he came to hide amongst the Amish to get away from the woman and avoid contributing to the child's upbringing."

Betsy studied the bishop's face and expected a disappointed look, instead she was sure she saw a hint of amusement on his face. Betsy sat in silence as she waited for him to reprimand her, or tell her how to make amends.

"Have you confessed your sin to *Gott*?"

Betsy nodded slowly. "*Jah*, I have."

The bishop spread his arms out, palms up. "Then *Gott* has forgiven you."

Betsy looked at the bishop in shock and hoped he wasn't going to add anything more, such as she would have to confess her wickedness in front of the congregation. When he remained silent, she said, "That's it?"

He leaned forward with his bottom jaw slightly protruding. "What did you want?"

"I don't know, I mean – I'm not sure. It's just that it was a wicked, horrible thing to do." Betsy chewed on her bottom lip. She almost wished she would have some sort of punishment, at least that might make her feel better. Maybe she would feel better if she did have to confess her sin to the whole congregation.

"*Gott* forgives us of all our unrighteousness if we confess our sins to Him and ask His forgiveness." The bishop smiled kindly. "Of course, you'll have to speak to Richard and confess to him what you've said about him."

A wave of nausea swept over Betsy. She would never have said such horrible things if she knew she would have to ask forgiveness for them. "Of course, I do, don't I."

"*Jah*, I think you know that you need to speak with him."

Betsy nodded. "*Denke* for hearing me."

Chapter 13

Now unto Him that is able to do exceeding

abundantly above all that we ask or think,

according to the power that worketh in us,

Unto Him be glory in the church by Christ Jesus

throughout all ages,

world without end. Amen

Ephesians 3:20-21

Richard opened the door of the buggy and Max immediately jumped out and ran off, sniffing the ground as he went.

"Don't worry about him. He won't go far," Jakob called out.

Richard looked up to see Jakob standing on the porch. "Hello, Jakob."

"Hello, come inside. Our other guest hasn't arrived yet."

As Richard walked toward Jakob, he asked, "So who is the mystery woman? Would it be someone I've already met?"

Richard hoped it wouldn't be Lucy. His date with Lucy had been a disaster and he did not want to spend another meal listening to her whining prattle about nothing. When Jakob didn't respond, Richard asked again, "So who did you say was also coming to dinner?"

"I'm under strict instructions that my lips are to be sealed."

"Abigail told you not to tell me?"

Jakob nodded.

Richard groaned. "I guess I'll find out soon enough."

Jakob laughed as they both stepped through the door. Just as they sat down, they heard the sound of another buggy pulling up.

Jakob jumped up. "I'll see her in."

Richard stayed on the couch, nervous about whom Abigail had coming to dinner. He hoped it would be someone he could have a conversation with and not someone young and silly.

"I believe you two know each other."

Richard stood to the sound of Jakob's voice. The woman was Betsy. "Good evening, Betsy."

"Hello, Richard. I'm sorry I had no idea that you were coming for dinner too."

"No need to apologize. I hope you still would've accepted the invitation if you knew I was coming."

Jakob stepped between the two of them. "I have no idea where Abigail is. I'll leave the two of you and find her."

Jakob promptly left the two of them alone. Richard wondered whether this was purely another ploy in their clumsy match making scheme.

'"I'm very sorry about this, Betsy. Would you rather me go?"

Betsy shook her head, and said, "*Nee*, why would I want you to go?"

"We haven't exactly got off to the best start. I'm surprised you're staying, quite frankly."

"It would be rude if one of us left. Don't you think so?" Betsy asked.

There was a silence for a time until, Betsy said, "I really like Abigail and Jakob, I wouldn't like to upset them by leaving. Let's just be polite to each other in front of them."

Richard dipped his head and scratched his forehead. "I guess we could be polite to each other, just while we're here."

Betsy shot him a quizzical look. He smiled and looked up at Abigail bustling through the back door.

"Hello, you two." Abigail's words were nearly breathless. "I got carried away in the herb garden." Abigail had a bunch of green herbs in her hand. "You two know each other, don't you?"

Richard knew very well that Abigail knew he knew Betsy. "*Jah*, we know each other."

Jakob followed Abigail in through the back door. "Sit both of you, please."

While Abigail took her herbs into the kitchen, Betsy and Richard were forced to sit next to each other on the couch.

Betsy gritted her teeth. "How's the *haus* going, Richard?"

"I'm part way through having the walls re-surfaced then I need to get a few spots fixed on the floor. Once I've done that, I'm going to call in an architect and try and bring the home back to how it would've looked."

Betsy looked down into her palms that were placed in her lap.

Jakob directed the conversation away from the *haus*. "How's the horse and buggy going?"

"*Jah, gut.* I've been following your instructions. I've been taking the buggy out every day and giving the horse a run, whether I need to go out or not." Richard turned to Betsy. "Let me know if you need to be driven anywhere, Betsy. I have a lot of free time."

Betsy smiled but her lips remained tight and rigid. "*Denke*, Richard. That's very kind of you."

Richard wondered how long their little charade of politeness would last before one of them let off steam at the other. He was going to do his very best to make sure it wasn't him who lost his temper first.

Once they were seated and eating dinner, Abigail spoke. "Betsy, I don't think that you know this, but I very nearly lost the businesses."

Betsy swallowed her mouthful of food, before she said, "Really?"

Abigail nodded. "*Jah*, and it was Richard who saved us from bankruptcy."

"How did he do that?" Betsy knew that Abigail and her late husband had opened a restaurant many years ago and they also had a B&B.

Abigail inhaled deeply. "It's a long story, we needed money and Richard lent me money for much lower than his usual rate. Not only that, he helped me with the business like a kind of a mentor. Even poured over the figures like an accountant and really whipped the businesses into shape."

Betsy studied Richard's face.

"You're too flattering, Abigail. I just gave a bit of guidance, that's all," Richard said.

"I was close to losing everything and you were there to help and I will never forget that," Abigail said.

When both Jakob and Abigail were out of the room fixing dessert, Betsy leaned close to Richard. "I need to speak to you privately."

"Is it important?"

Betsy nodded and was annoyed at his question. Why would she want to speak to him at all, if it weren't important? The sooner she could tell him the horrible thing she had done the better. Then she could be free of feeling badly and she could put Richard Black behind her.

"Do you want to speak to me tonight?"

Betsy nodded. "*Jah*."

"Follow me back to my *haus* when we leave here."

They finished their conversation just in time as Jakob and Abigail just came back in the room.

"I just realized the girls aren't here. Where are they?" Betsy said.

"They're staying with their *grossmammi* tonight. They stay there most every Saturday night as well," Jakob said.

Betsy noticed that Jakob shot Abigail a smile and she could only assume that they both relished a little quiet time when the girls were gone.

Chapter 14

I am crucified with Christ: nevertheless I live; yet not I, but Christ liveth in me: and the life which I now live in the flesh I live by the faith of the Son of God, who loved me, and gave himself for me.

Galatians 2:20

As planned, Betsy followed Richard back to his house when their dinner with Abigail and Jakob was over.

"Well, what did you want to speak with me about?" His tone was impatient, bordering on rude.

"I have a confession to make to you." Betsy knew that this would not be easy, given his obvious present state of mind.

Let's sit over here. He walked to the porch and sat on the step and once she sat beside him, he said, "Now go on."

"Well, you see …"

"Go on."

Betsy took a deep breath, exhaled slowly and wished her heart would stop pounding so much. "The thing is that I've said some terrible things about you."

Richard nodded. "And I, you."

"*Nee,* what I mean to say is, that I've told lies to people about you deliberately to make people think poorly of you."

"I see. You've been spreading rumors about me, is what you're trying to say?" Richard's sharp tone returned.

"*Jah.*" She hoped he would yell at her or tell her how awful she was for doing such a terrible thing.

"I already know that, but I appreciate you telling me."

"You know?"

"*Jah.*" Richard laughed. "You should know that you can't keep anything quiet in the community."

Betsy relaxed slightly. He didn't seem to be taking the news too badly at all.

"Betsy, I think we should call a truce."

"A what?"

"Truce. Its where two people stop their fighting."

Betsy looked out over the darkness of what was once her land. Although it was night, a nearly full moon lit up the fields under a blanket of twinkling stars. Could she stop fighting with the man who had taken all this land from her? "With this truce thing - we wouldn't have to be friends, would we?"

"You don't want to be friends with me?"

Betsy shook her head. She was only being truthful, she couldn't be friends, but she did not have to make an enemy out of the man.

"Okay, we won't be friends, but we shall call a truce. Which means we'll be nothing to each other. We'll be neutral toward one another, neither friend nor enemy." Richard put his hand out to shake her hand.

Betsy looked at him and considered what he said, then she put her hand in his.

Richard closed his large hand around hers. They looked into each other's eyes. Betsy was lost in his eyes as she felt her hand being pulled toward him. He was going to kiss her like they had kissed before. She closed her eyes for an instant, as his mouth moved to hers. She wanted to feel his lips on hers again and inhale his masculine scent.

"*Nee*." she pulled her hand from his at the last moment. She opened her eyes and jumped to her feet. "We can do the truce thing." She sat down again and looked straight into his face. "We'll be nothing to each other. We'll not be enemies, and we'll not be friends. Okay?"

Richard looked straight ahead and nodded.

Betsy stood up and without saying another word, and without looking back, she got into her *schweschder's* buggy and drove back home, back to her caravan.

****

Richard watched her leave, and scratched his neck agitatedly. *That woman has an effect on me like no other. She drives me wild in so many different ways*. He smiled as he thought, *she would never marry me – she can't stand the thought of me.*

As he waited for Betsy's buggy to make its way up his long driveway, away from him, he looked up at the *haus.* He would find as much history of the home as he could so he could pass on some of that knowledge to his *kinner* if he was ever blessed to have any.

****

The next day at the haberdashery store, Vida was determined to speak to Betsy. "I had a beau once."

Betsy looked up from the sewing machine. "You did?"

"*Jah,* I did. I was in love with him – very much so."

"What happened, if you don't mind me asking, Vida?"

"Pride got in the way. Is pride standing in your way?" The old lady bent down to look closely in Betsy's face.

"How do you mean, Vida?" Betsy stopped sewing and looked into the kind wrinkled face.

"You're too proud to admit that you're in love with him, aren't you."

"Vida." Milly's voice was loud and angry. "Leave Betsy alone she's trying to sew."

Once Vida was out of earshot, Milly whispered to Betsy. "I'm sorry she's been listening to local rumors about you and Richard Black."

Betsy smiled and nodded and wondered what rumors were circulating about the two of them. She considered what Vida said to her. Maybe that overwhelming feeling she had for Richard, was love. If only she wasn't also mad at him, then she might recognize if her feelings were love or something else.

Betsy decided that after work she should pay Richard a visit and see what would come of it. Just a friendly visit, as neighbors visit one another.

She was glad that she'd borrowed Grace's buggy that day; no one would know that she visited him.

Betsy tried not to look at her old *haus* when she pulled up outside it. It was too painful to think about let alone to look at the place that was once hers. She knocked on one of the large double doors at the front. No one answered, so she knocked once more. She was just about to give up and go home when Richard came around the corner.

"Betsy, I thought I heard someone knocking."

"Hello, Richard. I thought I'd visit."

Richard did not answer her; he just stood still.

"Visit you, as neighbors visit each other," she explained.

It was then that he smiled. "Come sit on the porch then. I've only just today got two porch chairs."

As they sat, Betsy had no idea what to say. She'd already apologized for the nasty things she'd done and said, what else was left to speak of? "I've started a new job."

"Where at?"

"Just at a haberdashery store." Betsy couldn't help but giggle when she thought of the two old ladies she worked for.

Richard stared at her with such scrutiny that Betsy immediately became very uncomfortable, and she again became silent.

"Betsy, I've never seen you laugh like that. You brighten the world with your laugh."

Betsy laughed a little, but nervously this time. "Brighten up the world? Surely that's an exaggeration."

"Let me rephrase, then. You brighten up my world."

Betsy swallowed hard against the lump that had developed in her throat. She looked away from him.

"I'm sorry, Betsy. I don't mean to be so forward, but you have an effect on me; an effect that no woman has ever had on me before."

Betsy stared at him. *Could it be that they were both in love with each other?*

"Betsy, I think that I have fallen in …"

"I must go." Betsy leaped off the chair and hurried to the buggy hoping that Richard would not follow. She untied the reins of the buggy and climbed in. Out of the corner of her eye, she could see that Richard had not followed her and had remained on the porch.

"Clk, clk, up, Chester." She clicked the large, bay horse forward and drove away from Richard to the safety of her small caravan.

****

I know she feels something for me too. I can see it in her eyes. Yet, it's too painful for me to stay around here, so close to her.

Richard decided to go away from Pennsylvania County, just for a couple of days and see if his feelings remained the same once he was away from the Amish and Betsy.

Chapter 15

Knowing that a man is not justified by the works of the law,

but by the faith of Jesus Christ, even we have believed in Jesus Christ, that we might be justified by the faith of Christ, and not by the works of the law:

for by the works of the law shall no flesh be justified.

Galatians 2:16

Once Betsy had unhitched the buggy and attended to Chester, she walked the small distance to her caravan. She flung the door open and threw herself on the bed.

I'm sure he was just about to say he loves me. Surely love doesn't happen so quickly. I've hardly known him for any time at all. Betsy realized she didn't know if love happened quickly or slowly. In fact, she knew nothing of love.

"Betsy, are you all right?"

Betsy got off the bed and opened the caravan door to the sound of Grace's voice. "Hi, Grace, *jah* I'm okay. Just visited someone after work that's why I'm a little late home."

"Who would you visit? I don't mean to sound rude, but you don't visit anyone – not that I've ever known about."

Betsy was not in the mood to take offence, besides, she needed her *schweschder's* advice. "I visited Richard, next door. I think I'm in love with him."

"Really? I thought you didn't like him."

"That was because of the *haus*. Do you think that I could really be in love with him?"

"*Jah*, of course he's a very handsome *mann,* and I hear that he's also kind."

Betsy sat back on one of the two-seater bench at the side of the caravan. "But this is me, Grace. I don't think I've ever been in love and I don't know what it feels like. Tell me what it's like."

Grace sat next to her and a beaming smile covered her face. "It's like nothing else in the world matters when you're with that person. It's like when you are with them, you feel that you're home. It just feels right. That's all I can say."

Betsy considered what Grace had said. She did *feel good to* be around him and she wanted to be close to him all the time. She even wanted to kiss him, and she had never ever wanted to kiss any other man.

Grace leaned forward, "Why so quiet? Did you think you'd never love anyone?"

Betsy nodded because she was too frightened to say so, out aloud. "Maybe I've ruined things, Grace. I think he was just about to tell me that he likes me or even loves me, and I ran away from him."

Grace stroked Betsy's arm. "If he likes you, he won't give up that easily. *Menner* like to chase women. They like to feel they've worked hard to get their *fraa*."

Betsy giggled. “You make it sound like a game.”

“*Nee*, more like a sport,” Grace said, and then she tossed back her head and laughed.

Betsy was a little calmer about everything, but she still did not know what should come next. Maybe she would wait for him to do something since she visited him last – maybe she should wait for him to visit her. If love was a sport, or even a game, then the next move was definitely his.

Chapter 16

I am crucified with Christ: nevertheless I live; yet not I, but Christ liveth in me: and the life which I now live in the flesh I live by the faith of the Son of God, who loved me, and gave himself for me.

Galatians 2:20

The next afternoon, Grace collected Betsy from work and was taking her home when they both saw smoking billowing near their home. "That's not your home is it, Grace?"

"I hope not, I've been out most of the day. If it's not my *haus*, it's very near it."

"Probably my caravan," Betsy said, thinking that might be her punishment for being so awful. Maybe she should have been grateful for what she had instead of looking what she didn't have.

If the caravan had gone up in flames she would be forced to inconvenience Grace and her husband by staying in their tiny *haus.* Suddenly, she was grateful for the blessing of her caravan where she had a little privacy and was not inconveniencing anyone.

"*Nee*, I think it's coming from your old *haus*."

"*Nee*, it couldn't be." Betsy tugged on Grace's arm. "Go that way and see, Grace."

"*Jah*, I was going to."

As Betsy's old house came into view, they saw two fire engines and large hoses pouring water on huge flames galloping through the roof of old Blough home.

"Pull the horse up here, we'll go on foot."

They tied the horse to a fence rail and ran to the house. There were a group of neighbors trying to help put out the fire, and the firemen told them to keep away.

Betsy scanned the crowd and couldn't see Richard anywhere. Then she saw Jakob. She ran to him. "Jakob, where's Richard."

Jakob's face was black and sweat was pouring from his brow, he was hardly recognizable. "They can't find him anywhere."

"Could he still be in the *haus*?"

Just then, two firemen came running out of the *haus* and Betsy heard one of them say, "We've done all we can to contain it."

Betsy ran to one of the firemen. "Could anyone still be in there?"

"Get back, lady." The fireman yelled at her.

Betsy ran to another of the fireman who was closer to the truck. "No one knows where the owner is."

The fireman shook his head. "Half the place was destroyed when we got here. We've done all we can and there was no sign of anyone."

Jakob put his arm around her shoulder. "His horse is still here. I've let him out into the paddock in case the barn catches alight as well."

It wasn't good that his horse was there. It meant that he wasn't out anywhere.

"What if he's in there, Jakob?"

Jakob lowered his head. “We just have to hope that he isn’t.”

Grace stood next to her and put an arm around her waist. They stood a safe distance from the *haus* and watched the cruel flames leap into the air and the black smoke darken the late afternoon sky.

Betsy was sick to her stomach. She had been so worried about losing her house and now she realized that it was nothing – it was just a building. She whispered to Grace, “He had to be in there, where else would he be? His horse is still here.”

Grace kept quiet and held her tighter. After a while, Grace said, “Come on, we can’t watch this. Let’s go home.”

Chapter 17

That the trial of your faith, being much more precious than of gold that perisheth, though it be tried with fire, might be found unto praise and honour and glory at the appearing of Jesus Christ:

1 Peter 1:7

Tears trickled down Betsy's as Grace led her back to the buggy. They traveled the short distance in silence.

"You must have dinner with us tonight, Betsy," Grace said as she led the horse to the stable.

"*Nee*, I couldn't possibly eat; I just want to be alone."

Grace left her alone and Betsy closed the door of her caravan. She'd lost her house that had once meant everything, now she hoped she hadn't lost Richard as well.

Where could he be if he wasn't in the haus? He couldn't have gone far without his buggy, and if he'd gone for a walk, he would've seen the flames. Max wasn't anywhere to be seen, but Max would've most likely run away from the fire, once it started. Every possible scenario ran through Betsy's mind until she fell asleep, exhausted.

The next morning, Betsy had to go to work. Grace drove her past the *haus.* Everything had burned to the ground and there was no sign of anyone, and Richard's horse was still in the paddock.

"I've got a little time before work. Let's go to Abigail and Jakob's place. Maybe they've learned more of things."

Grace drove to Abigail and Jakob's *haus*, but they had no more information on Richard. All they knew was that the fire experts were to inspect the property later that day to determine the cause of the fire.

"I can't go to work today, Grace. Please take me home."

"Of course, Betsy. No one would expect you to go to work. I'll take you home, and then I'll go and tell the ladies that you can't work today. I'm sure they'll understand."

"*Denke*, Grace."

Once back in her caravan, Betsy took off her prayer *kapp* and slumped onto her bed and just lay there. Numbness wracked her body as she remembered Richard and how his smile made her heart beat faster, how his lips felt against hers.

She sat straight up in bed when she heard scratching at her door. She opened the door to see Max. "Max."

"You're not stealing my dog again, are you?"

Betsy looked up to see Richard. Tears flooded from her eyes and spilled down her face. As Richard stepped closer to her, she collapsed into his arms.

"I'm sorry about the *haus*," he said. "I got the shock of my life when the taxi drove me where the house used to be this morning. I thought he'd taken a wrong turn. I've just finished speaking with the fire department, and the police."

"Don't worry, it's just a *haus*." She looked into his eyes. "I was so worried, I thought that you might have died in the fire. Where were you?"

"Max and I had to get away for a day or two to clear our heads. Did you say that you were worried about me?"

Betsy looked into his dark eyes and nodded. "Richard, you can't go away and leave a horse in a stable."

"He had plenty of food and water, and I wasn't gone long."

Betsy shook her head. "Don't do it again."

"I won't. I'll learn to do things properly." Richard wiped the tears away from her face and then held her tightly. "It feels *gut* to have you in my arms." They held each other tightly for a moment, and then Richard said, "Betsy, I think we should get married."

Betsy pulled apart from him a little and opened her mouth, but she could not speak.

"I can't stop thinking about you," he said, by way of explanation.

Betsy managed a little laugh. "What happens one day if you *do* stop thinking about me?"

"Then I will be loving you and caring for you, and doing everything to make sure that you're happy." He took hold of Betsy's hand. "You see, from the moment I first saw you – that time you kicked dirt at me with your little black, lace up boots, I've not been able to stop thinking about you." Richard shrugged. "There is something about you – some essence within you that draws me to you like a hungry bee to a fragrant flower."

Betsy put a hand to her chest, she was overwhelmed at his words. Her instinct was to laugh, but she could not draw a breath.

"Betsy, say you'll marry me, or I don't know what I'll do."

Betsy looked into Richard's eyes and the annoyance that was once in her heart, had gone, and in its place was a feeling she'd never known. She too had a driving compulsion to be near him; could this be the thing called love? As she stared into Richard Black's hopeful eyes, another tear trickled down her cheek. "I want to say yes, but I feel that I don't know much about you."

"I'll tell you all about myself. What would you like to know first?"

"Where are your parents and do you have any brothers and sisters?"

"My parents died years ago and I have a brother." He sighed.

"Do you want *kinner*?"

"*Jah*, I would like to have *kinner*. I'd like my *haus* to be filled with laughter, happiness and lots of *kinner*."

"Will you marry me? The bishop says we should get married."

"The bishop?" Richard laughed. "*Jah*, I told him how I was annoyed and angry and he guessed I was speaking of a woman, and said that I should marry you. Maybe he was joking – I'm not certain."

Betsy laughed. "I went to the bishop too, to confess how horrible I'd been to you." She realized that Richard had only seen her at her worst and still he wanted to marry her. Betsy considered the pain she had experienced when she thought he had gone for good and the joy she felt now that he was in her arms.

She did not want to let him go ever again. She took a deep breath, and said, "We should court first, and then see what happens." Grace's words rang through her head that menner want to work for their *fraa* – she did want to make him wait just a little while.

"You're a stubborn woman, Betsy." He rested his head on hers, squeezed her tightly, and said, "I'll build us another *haus*, exactly the same as the old one."

"The *haus* doesn't matter anymore, as long as you're safe. What was the cause of the fire?"

"They're still trying to work out what started it. They've ruled out arson."

"You mean someone who deliberately lit it?" A wicked thought crossed Betsy's mind. *Did Richard light the fire so there would be nothing to stand in their way? Surely not.* She dismissed the thought just as quickly as it had arrived.

"*Jah.* It can't have been an electrical fault because no electricity or wires were in the *haus*. That's the most common cause of house fires, you know. Maybe I didn't put the fire out properly before I left." He shook his head. "Who knows."

"Where are you going to stay?"

"At Jakob's and Abigail's place, I guess. It might take a while for the house to be rebuilt." Richard held Betsy at arms length and looked down into her eyes. "So can we say that we are officially courting – engaged?"

Betsy nodded, and Richard scooped her up in his strong arms and swung her around until they were both dizzy. Richard fell to the ground with Betsy in his arms.

"You know, we're going to get married one day, don't you, Betsy?"

Betsy smiled and said, "My *haus* – our *haus* brought us together."

As they both lay in the long grass, Richard said, "Would you like to be married in our *haus,* as soon as I rebuild it?"

Betsy dug him in the ribs. "I haven't said, 'yes,' yet."

Richard laughed, "As good as, if we're engaged. I think you have said 'yes.' Anyway, at some point in the future, would you like to get married in our *haus*?"

Betsy smiled and nodded. "*Jah*, I would."

Richard stood up and pulled Betsy to her feet. "My life has meaning now that I've found *Gott* and become Amish. I'm glad I made the simple change."

"I'm glad you did too, and I'm glad you bought my *haus*." As Richard held Betsy in his arms she couldn't help, but consider how *Gott* could turn a disaster such as losing her *haus,* into something even better, such as finding a husband who was kind and whose heart was right toward *Gott.*

Whither shall I go from thy Spirit? Or whither shall I flee from thy presence?
If I ascend up into heaven, thou art there.
If I take the wings of the morning, and dwell in the uttermost parts of the sea; Even there shall thy hand lead m, and thy right hand shall hold me.
Psalm 139:7-10

The End

****

Thank you for your interest in
'*A Simple Change*' the last book in the
Amish Wedding Season series.

To keep up to date on

Samantha Price's new releases

and giveaways subscribe at:

http://www.samanthapriceauthor.com

****

Connect with Samantha at:

samanthaprice333@gmail.com

http//twitter.com/AmishRomance

Made in the USA
Charleston, SC
10 February 2017